KILTY AS SIN

KILTY SERIES: BOOK FOUR

Amy Vansant

CHAPTER ONE

Six Months Ago

Peter felt the man before he saw him.

He, his buddy Dean and their boss, Volkov, sat stage-side at the Minty Minx strip club, watching a sleepy-eyed redhead loll through her pole routine. It wouldn't have surprised Peter if she'd stopped to check her text messages in the middle of the dance. Though, he couldn't imagine where she'd keep her phone.

A redheaded stripper named *Ginger*. She hadn't shown any effort in picking a stage name, either.

Nothing kept Dean from checking his phone. He'd been texting back and forth with someone since they arrived. Volkov only had eyes for Ginger. Peter spent half his time watching the girl and the other half staring at the wall opposite her. Dean had found Peter the job with Volkov only a few days earlier, so Peter felt obligated to look grateful for the free trip to the strip joint.

In truth, it wasn't his thing.

The job paid well—Volkov was some kind of Russian gangster, although Dean said he wasn't connected to the real Russian mob—he was a lone wolf. Dean said that was funny because that's what Volkov's name meant. *Wolf*.

Dean had implied it was the mob who didn't want Volkov and not the other way around, but Peter didn't care. He was a bit of a Russian mutt, on his mother's side.

The job had come just in time. Peter needed the money. He'd done three months in High Desert State Prison for drug possession with intent to distribute—though he'd had no intent to sell. The meth was all for him.

He got clean in prison and, following his early release for good behavior, Dean said he could take over *his* job. The position watching over Volkov's safe house came with room and board, so it solved all of Peter's post-prison problems.

Dean packed up and moved out of Volkov's safe house two seconds after Peter walked through the door. "Good luck," he'd said. Peter hadn't loved his tone, or the little chuckle that followed, but he figured, *how bad could it be?*

Free rent was free rent.

His gaze following Ginger's travels down the pole, Dean stood and slipped his phone back into his pocket. He slapped Volkov on the back and said something to him. Volkov nodded, his attention never leaving Ginger.

A quick nod to Peter and Dean left. Peter glanced at Volkov. It seemed they'd be staying.

Peter returned to watching Ginger rub her cheek against the pole. Not her rear cheeks, but her *face* cheek. It hit him as odd. He suspected she was trying to grab a quick nap.

That's when he *felt* a presence in the chair left empty by Dean's absence. He turned, thinking Dean had returned, but it wasn't his buddy. The man sitting between them now was taller and thinner.

The man glanced in his direction, revealing eyes so light blue they looked white. A black edge rimmed the man's pale irises but Peter only caught a brief glimpse. The man looked away as if Peter wasn't worth considering.

Dick.

Volkov and the stranger talked. From the bits and pieces Peter overheard, he couldn't tell if the two men knew each other or not.

"I like to take them home," Volkov screamed over the throbbing music.

"It would be nice to keep them and pull them out when you want a dance, huh?" said the man.

Peter looked at White-Eyes, expecting him to be chuckling at his stupid joke, but he wasn't. He stared at Ginger with those crazy eyes. Serious as cancer.

Something made Peter's neck shiver and he bunched his shoulders against the cold.

"It's harder than you think," said Volkov, laughing.

Peter relaxed a little. The fact Volkov laughed made

everything seem more normal.

Except...

He'd been at Volkov's safe house for two nights. Someone had torn out the main bathroom and refashioned it as an empty, windowless, oversized closet. The room gave Peter the creeps, both because it reminded him of his cell back at High Desert and because it wasn't *right*. He'd asked Dean what it was for and Dean said, "It's Volkov's. You want the job or not?"

So, he'd let it drop.

"Basements make good sound dampeners."

Peter looked at White-Eyes again.

What did he just say?

Peter couldn't shake the uneasiness creeping along his scalp. He was no women's libber—he'd made his share of off-color jokes. But something about the way Volkov and White-Eyes were talking about captive women—it sounded more like a scientific discussion than fantasy banter.

It sounded like a *plan*.

Peter concentrated on Ginger's freckled breasts, but a sudden, inexplicable vision of himself digging a basement through the hard Nevada caliche filled his brain. He had an abrupt urge to leap up, buy pickaxes and shovels, and start digging.

For Ginger.

As he watched the girl sway to the music, Peter realized he wanted to put *Ginger* in the hole.

Not any hole.

The hole *he* dug.

Peter rubbed his hand across his head as if he were trying to raise a genie from his skull.

What the hell is wrong with me?

He'd never had thoughts like that in his life.

Peter felt a movement at his elbow and turned to see White-Eyes standing to leave.

Thank God.

As the thin man moved away, he banged into Peter with his right arm. His flesh was hard. It felt as though someone had bumped into him with a bat.

Peter glanced at Volkov. The Russian watched Ginger.

Peter did the same.

After a bit, he felt better. He pushed the image of himself digging holes from his mind and watched Volkov hand Ginger a stack of money. Not stripper money. *Real money*. Ginger nodded, talking with Volkov.

Peter couldn't hear what they were talking about.

It didn't hit him as odd when he found himself driving Volkov and Ginger back to the safe house. He'd hoped he'd be dropping the two of them off at Volkov's real house, but the Russian had muttered the address of the safe house to him as he and the girl slid into the backseat.

Peter heard the two of them mumbling as he drove. Ginger wasn't a giggler. Her personality didn't perk *off* stage, either.

When they arrived at the safe house, Ginger wandered into the kitchen muttering something about sparkling water.

'Cause she's so fancy.

Volkov opened the linen closet and pulled out a black tote bag Peter had never noticed before. Volkov took the bag into the cell room, before leading the girl to the bag and shutting the door behind them.

Peter stood there, staring at the closed door, unsure what he was supposed to do while his boss had sex in a jail cell with a stripper. On either side of the cell room were bedrooms. Why would he take her into the empty cell?

When the screaming started, Peter turned up the television and sat on the sofa. The walls of the cell were hard, like cement, and the door had been reinforced with strips of thick wood, but Peter still heard the screaming.

It didn't sound like sex screaming.

Every so often the door would rattle as if someone had thrown themselves against it.

Peter turned up the volume again. After another ten minutes, he grabbed a bottle of vodka from the kitchen. He wasn't supposed to drink, but...it's not like it was *meth*. He poured himself a large shot and then another.

Peter carried the bottle back to the sofa.

Peter opened his eyes. He'd fallen asleep. He looked at the cell door to find it cracked open.

"Volkov?"

He must have left.

The bottle of vodka sitting on the table beside him was nearly empty. Was he supposed to be keeping watch?

I hope I'm not in trouble.

Peter turned down the television and stood, staring at the cell door. He crossed the four feet to the entrance and was about to peek inside when the door swung open. Ginger stumbled past, pushing him, nearly knocking him over on her way toward the front door. Her face was swollen and covered in blood.

She pushed open the screen door and ran out of the house, screaming. A second later Peter heard the screeching of tires and a thump.

The screaming stopped.

"Go see."

Peter jumped. Volkov stood behind him, his body naked but for a pair of wrestling shorts, his tattooed skin glistening with sweat and blood.

"What?" he asked. His mind felt like a seized motor.

Volkov grabbed and squeezed his arm before pushing him toward the front door. *"Go find her."*

Peter followed in Ginger's footsteps. People gathered on the road outside the house. A man stood over the form of a red-headed girl, her twisted body illuminated in the headlights of his Impala.

Ginger's left leg bent at an unnatural angle. Her body was covered in scrapes. She wasn't naked, which struck Peter as the oddest thing of all.

"She came out of nowhere." The man hovering over her repeated the phrase over and over. People around them announced they were calling 911.

Peter turned and reentered the house. He found his boss in the cell room.

Volkov had thrown on one of Peter's t-shirts. In his hand hung a bucket, an orange sponge floating in the murky water. The room looked as it always did, but for the smell of disinfectant.

Volkov thrust the bucket at him. "Dump this down the sink and put the bucket underneath."

Peter took the bucket and did as he was told. The water appeared light red against the white sink as it swirled down the drain.

When he returned to the living room, Volkov tossed his t-shirt at him. He had slipped back into the black oxford he'd been wearing at the club.

"I wasn't here," said the Russian.

Peter nodded.

Volkov pushed past him, walking through the kitchen toward the back door, pausing on the porch off the back. He tapped his toe on the ground and then looked back at Peter.

"Tomorrow go out and get some shovels and pickaxes. Things to dig."

Peter nodded.

"Puttin' in a pool?" he asked.

He wasn't sure why he'd said it.

He knew they wouldn't be digging a pool.

CHAPTER TWO

Broch cocked his head as he passed Studio Twelve. It sounded as if thunder bounced inside the huge metal building. Curious, he opened the door and let the cacophony wash over him.

Applause.

Not thunder at all.

People haein a guid time.

Broch wandered in and stood behind two men posted at the top of a set of stairs leading down to a stage. The men turned as he entered and, recognizing him as a fellow Parasol Pictures staffer, nodded. Both their attentions dropped to his kilt and then darted away.

Broch straightened and pushed out his chest.

Aye. That's richt. It's a kilt day.

Catriona had been trying for weeks to crack his pattern of kilt-wearing days vs. pants-wearing days, but truth be told, even he didn't know what inspired him to don the kilt in which he'd arrived in the twenty-first century. Maybe he felt a little extra homesick on the days he wore the kilt. Who could blame him? He'd moved five thousand miles and nearly three centuries from ancient Scotland to modern-day Los Angeles. He'd traveled from cool, green countryside to cold metal, hot sand, and burning pavement. He liked the sun well enough in small doses. The palm trees were pretty, and of course, he loved Catriona—but he deserved to be a little sentimental for his homeland once in a while.

On wistful days he wore the kilt. Then there were the days he wore the kilt for no other reason but to send Catriona into a tailspin wondering *why* he'd worn the kilt.

This was one of those days.

It made him chuckle thinking about her eyes widening at the sight of him, her lips pressing into that adorable little sandwich of frustration...

She made a mistake letting me ken she wis trying tae figure mah pattern.

But as eager as he was to saunter by Catriona, at the moment, he couldn't take his attention from the television show being filmed below him. He watched the four women gabbing from their flower-print sofa perches, white lights trained on them from the scaffolding above. He heard their voices over the speakers in the room. The path leading to them, down wide stairs, was lined with people sitting in plastic chairs.

The clappers.

No, Catriona called them something else—

The studio audience.

Broch recognized the women below him from the television in his apartment. It fascinated him to see them in real life, full-sized and truly alive. While he'd come to understand the *concept* of television, it still felt a little like magic to him. Even Catriona had been unable to explain to him how the picture box worked. Something about images beaming through space—

"Who else has a love problem they'd like to share with us?" asked a tiny Asian woman from her corner of the sofa.

Niko. Broch remembered her name.

A woman from the audience stood and worked her way through the crowd to the stairs as the others clapped and hooted. She approached a standing microphone not far from the stage and tucked an errant hair behind her ear.

"My husband won't stop leaving his bath towels on the ground."

In unison, a grumble rose from the crowd and Broch watched the largely female audience nod their heads as if they, too, were married to the same towel-dropping husband.

Broch scratched his chin, trying to remember where he'd put his bath towel that morning.

Oan the hook oan the back o' the door.

He'd assumed that's what the hook was for. Maybe this woman's husband didn't know where the hook was?

"Dae ye hae a hook?" he asked aloud.

Heads in the audience turned to him. The woman complaining about her husband followed the stares of the others and peered up at Broch.

"Oh *my*," said one of the talky women in their microphone It echoed through the studio as giggling rose from the crowd.

"What's that sir? Can you come this way a bit?" asked a heavyset black woman from her spot beside Niko. She flashed long violet-painted nails at him as she motioned for him to come forward.

Broch recognized her as TeeTee. She was his favorite. She made him laugh out loud in his apartment.

"Me?" he asked, placing a hand on his chest. He wore his new favorite t-shirt, white with the printed image of a shaggy brown Highland bull in the center of it. Catriona had bought it for him. He'd suspected it might be lucky and here he was, singled out by TeeTee.

TeeTee motioned to him again, nodding. "Come down where we can see you better."

Broch wandered down the stairs toward the mic. The woman standing there stepped away so he could take her place, but as he moved in, she slipped her arm around his waist.

"Is he my parting gift?" she asked.

The studio exploded with laughter.

TeeTee rolled her eyes. "No, you cannot keep that man. You sit yourself down."

Cackling with laughter, the woman smacked Broch on the butt before making her way back to her seat. The audience erupted with giggles a second time as Broch jumped, shocked by the feel of a hand on his posterior.

He hooked his mouth to the side. He'd had to take a class on sexual harassment for his job with the studio, and in the training video, when the man patted the *woman's* behind, warning alarms had sounded.

"Now, you were saying, sir?" prompted TeeTee, flashing the ass-paddling woman one last disapproving glare.

Broch faced forward and cleared his throat. He glanced to his left and then his right.

It felt as if everyone was staring at him.

"Em... Whit?"

His voice boomed over the speakers and he snapped back his neck to look skyward. He leaned toward the mic again.

"Hullo?"

His voice echoed through the studio and he grinned, singing softly.

"You'll take the high road and I'll take the low road,
And I'll be in Scotland afore you.
Where me and my true love will never meet again,
On the bonnie, bonnie banks of Loch Lomond—
Ho, ho mo leannan
Ho mo leannan bhoidheach..."

He'd expected the audience to join in during the last bit, but they only stared at him. Pulling back from the mic, he sniffed and smoothed his kilt before trying again.

"Ah'm sorry. Whit did ye want noo?"

"Tell us what you wanted to tell us," prompted TeeTee. "When you were up there. Before you started singing."

Broch realized he didn't remember what had brought him down the stairs.

"Er..."

"You said something about the man's bath towel?"

"Oh. Och. Aye." He lifted his arm to run a hand through his hair as whispers erupted to his right. Ladies were pointing at his arm. He lowered it.

"Uh...I hae a hook oan mah door. Tis whaur ah hing mah towel. Ah thought mibbie the lady's husband didnae ken 'twas thare..."

The audience broke into applause, mixed with a heavy dose of laughing and murmuring as they worked together to translate his brogue.

The blonde on stage lifted a magazine from the coffee table in front of her and began to fan herself.

"Kimmee, what are you doing?" asked TeeTee.

The woman closed her eyes. "I'm imagining him in a towel..."

More laughing. Broch felt his cheeks grow warm. He began to raise his hand to his head again and then stopped, remembering the reaction it had inspired the first time. Instead, he rubbed his knuckles. He didn't know what to do with his hands.

Niko motioned for quiet. "So you're saying she should make it *easy* for her husband to hang the towel."

Broch leaned to the mic, his lips brushing the rough metal. "Aye. Git him a hook."

Niko nodded. "That's good advice. What's your name?"

"Brochan."

"There's nothing broken about *that*," mumbled Kimmee into her mic, much to the delight of the audience.

"Where are you from, Brochan?" continued Niko.

"Scootlund."

The audience began murmuring again.

"Do you have a *love* question of your own for us?"

"A loue quaistion?"

The audience urged him to share.

"Are you in a relationship, Brochan?" asked TeeTee.

"Please say no!" screamed someone from the audience.

A ripple of laughter ran through the room.

Broch chewed on his lip. "Aye. Ah think ah am."

"Awww..." said the audience.

TeeTee pursed her lips and crossed her arms against her chest. "I was going to ask him if anything is confusing about his relationship, but I think we can all agree he sounds pretty confused."

The audience clapped, giving Broch a moment to collect his thoughts.

Mibbee ah dae hae a quaistion.

There *had* been something bothering him in his personal life.

He leaned into the mic again. "Mah wummin doesn't wantae git merrit."

His voice boomed back at him, quieting the audience.

"Your girlfriend doesn't want to get married?" asked Niko.

"You snooze you lose," said Kimmie, pretending to stand as if she was going to claim him as her own.

TeeTee put a hand on Kimmie's knee to settle her. "Why doesn't she want to marry you?"

Broch sighed. "She says she wants tae huv a go me foremaist."

The three other women scowled, but TeeTee sat up straight, slapping the seat beside her with her palm. "Honey, you aren't the easiest thing to understand so forgive me if I heard this wrong, but are you saying she wants to have sex with you first? Try out the merchandise, so to speak?"

Broch felt his cheeks grow warm. "Aye."

The audience gasped and hooted.

"And you don't want to?"

Kimmie held out a hand. "Wait. Is she not your *type*? You're not leading that girl on are you?"

Broch didn't understand her question. "Eh?"

"Well, you are wearing a skirt..."

The audience laughed as Broch scowled. "Tis nae ah *skirt.* Tis ah *kilt.*"

Kimmie cocked an eyebrow. "I think you know what I'm saying."

"He is in *awfully* good shape," mumbled Niko.

Broch grimaced, unsure where to go. "Ahm waantin' her tae be mah *wife.*"

TeeTee pointed at him with a violet nail. "But, you're saving yourself for marriage?"

Broch put his hand on his chest. "Nae *me.*"

"Who then? *Her?* You're saving *her* for marriage?"

The audience gasped.

A crash echoed from the back of the studio. Heads turned, including Broch's.

Catriona appeared at the top of the stairs, out of breath, the doors behind her bouncing off the walls before shutting. The two bouncers split to allow her access to the stairs. Spotting all attention pointed in her direction, she grimaced before hustling down the stairs.

Broch grinned. "Guid day, Catriona."

Catriona slipped on a stair, caught herself on the back of a chair, apologized to the woman sitting there for clipping her ear, and then jogged the remaining steps to wrap her hands around Broch's arm. "What are you doing on set?" she hissed tugging him back up toward the door.

"The man coudnae fin' his towel hook and ah—"

"Excuse me." TeeTee's voice echoed through the studio. Catriona stopped tugging and turned to the stage, her expression pinched.

"Where do you think you're taking that man?"

"I'm sorry TeeTee, he works for me, er, Parasol Pictures. He's new."

"Are you his girlfriend?" asked Niko.

The crowd hushed, awaiting an answer.

Catriona looked at Broch and then back at Niko. "Um, what?"

"Are you his *girlfriend*? The one who wants to try him on for size before you get married?"

Kimmee shook a finger at her, grinning. "You're *naughty,*

girl."

The crowd exploded with laughter, clapping.

Broch had never seen Catriona turn that particular shade of red.

"Uh..."

She glared at the large cameras pointed at them. Looking down, she spoke in a low tone. Broch could barely make out what she said over the exuberant crowd.

"If you never do another thing for me, you will follow me out of here right now."

Catriona smiled and held up a hand before heading up the stairs. "Sorry for the interruption."

Broch watched her go and then hurried after her.

"Where are you going? Don't go," said one of the ladies behind him. It sounded like Kimmee, but he didn't turn.

The crowd called to them both, begging them not to leave as they made their way up the stairs and out the door into the Los Angeles sun.

As soon as they cleared the studio, Catriona threw her back against the wall of the building and slid to a squat, her head in her hands.

"We're going to have to discuss privacy and crashing shows and—" She looked up, her attention locked on his kilt.

"Why are you wearing *that*?"

Broch grinned.

CHAPTER THREE

"Queens over nines."

Tyler Bash smiled, revealing his cards. He'd been on a losing streak. The worst losing streak since he lost almost five thousand dollars to his college roommate a few years previously.

Five thousand didn't seem like much now. He *wished* he was down five thousand. He'd done the quick math in his head after the last hand and between last week and now, he owed the house nearly eighty thousand dollars.

Just saying the number in his head had knocked the wind out of him.

But queens and nines will pull me from the brink.

This would be the hand that reversed his luck. After he'd won the cherry role of *Ionic*, the boy superhero, in Parasol Pictures' comic book franchise movie, he *swore* he'd never be broke again. When he received his first check, he *knew* he'd never be broke again.

He'd never seen so many zeros.

He'd spend most of his first check on his new Hollywood Hills mansion. He'd paid off his college loans, too, to prove to his mom he could be trusted with his own money.

Right.

Feeling flush with what was left, he'd gone a little crazy with his poker-betting. Unfortunately, that *flush* feeling never reproduced itself in his cards.

He needed this win.

He glanced at his hand and tried to hide his excitement.

Act like you've been there.

Nope. *Can't.* Maybe it was the bourbon, or maybe he wasn't *that* good of an actor, but he felt too giddy to hide his recently whitened teeth. He reached for the pot.

"Just a second there, new blood."

Robert Williams, star of stage and screen, sat across from him, his cards still hidden, resting against his chest.

Tyler felt the blood drain from his cheeks.

No.

The old man unfurled a grin of his own. The tips of his gray mustache were tinged with yellow from cigarettes, but his teeth were as white and fake as his own.

Robert Williams looked like a cagey old lion about to steal dinner from the young cub.

No. No, no no...

Tyler felt bile rise in his throat. His arms remained outstretched, his hands flanking the pot.

Please no.

The old man laid down his cards.

"Kings over threes."

There they were. Three kings lording over his Queens.

The other players, all movie stars, erupted into jeers.

"That's going to hurt," said Fiona Duffy, pushing her cards toward the center of the table. She'd been the one to introduce Tyler to the room. He'd told her he liked to play poker and she'd told him about the celebrity game. He'd been so excited to play—*how had things gone so wrong?*

Tyler tried to move but his body wouldn't listen. Robert pushed his hands aside, the big, gaudy ring on the old man's right hand scraping against Tyler's sweaty palms.

"I'll take that."

Robert scooped the chips from between Tyler's hands and, with a wink, began stacking them.

"Sorry, kid."

No. No, no, no...

It took a moment, but Tyler found the ability to move again. He tried to blow off his loss with a joke, but his mouth felt too dry—he coughed while trying to speak. Leaning back, he dragged his frozen arms with him until he found a way to bend them at the elbows and put them in his lap.

Again, he did the math in his head.

One hundred and thirty-seven thousand dollars.

That's how much he owed the house.

I don't have one hundred and thirty-seven thousand dollars.

Technically, he'd been in debt before he even walked into the celebrity game, but the group knew the part he'd won. Comic book movie money was nothing to sneeze at. Fiona had cleared the way for him with the regulars.

I was so excited...

He glanced at Fiona and she shrugged, her lips pressed tight, head dipping sideways-right toward her bobbing shoulder. How she'd managed to say *sucks to be you—maybe next time, idiot* with a gesture of her body he wasn't sure, but he'd heard it as loud as if she'd screamed it in his face.

One hundred and thirty-seven thousand dollars is nothing to these people.

Tyler's attention roamed the table from the sitcom star to his left to the sports hero on his right, taking in every Hollywood icon in between.

What was I thinking?

He didn't belong with these people—people he'd grown up watching on television.

Who do I think I am?

A brief flash of nerves chilled his skin as he realized the stars sitting at the table with him weren't even the scariest things in the room.

His gaze rolled in the direction of the people sitting on the outskirts of the room. A big man with slicked-back black hair and spider's web tattoos sat next to Dez, a petite woman with a hard expression. Next to them sat a tall, gaunt man with cheeks hollow as a corpse's. He wore a black glove on his right hand. Tyler had no idea why.

The ghoul's ice blue eyes stared back at him.

Tyler looked away.

He'd *thought* Blue-eyed Skeletor had arrived with Fiona, but the way he stared—now he felt certain the ghoul had to be security for Alain, the Frenchman who owned the game.

There was *one* good thing about all three heavies sitting in the room with them.

They're all in the same place.

He needed to go elsewhere.

Tyler tapped the edge of the table with his fingertips, trying to look as casual as possible.

"Deal me out of this one, I'm going to hit the little boy's room."

He flashed his most charming smile and caught Dez watching him.

Distract her.

"Can I get a vodka, rocks?"

Sans smile, Dez nodded.

Smooth. That was a nice touch. Now everyone knew he'd be back for the vodka.

But he wouldn't be.

Hell, no.

He intended to be a distant memory before the ice even started melting in that vodka.

Tyler stepped into the hallway and took one step toward the bathrooms before scampering on his tippy-toes down the hall to the back door. Holding his breath, he tried the knob.

Please, please, please—

It turned.

Thank you, Jesus.

He cracked open the door, slipped outside onto a wooden deck, and hurried down the steps.

Heart ping-ponging inside his chest, Tyler turned the corner of the building and entered the alley between Jay's Joint and a donut shop. His car was parked out front. It was a Volvo. He'd kept the car his parents had handed down to him.

How mature was that?

He *was* capable of making smart decisions. He *didn't* buy the Maserati he'd wanted so badly.

All good decisions from now on.

I'll never put myself in this position again.

No more playing poker with the big dogs.

No gambling. No drugs...except a little weed. No drinking past midnight except at really massive parties...

He glanced up and saw the lit window where the game was playing on the second floor of Jay's. He hugged the building a little tighter.

He already felt better. He could see his trusty Volvo on the street. Tomorrow would be a new day.

First, he had to pay off his debts. Alain was a reasonable guy. He had to be. The people at his poker games were *famous.* He couldn't just knock them off or break their knees. There would be press. Paparazzi and whatnot.

Tonight he'd go home and get a good night's sleep. Then tomorrow, he'd make arrangements to repay Alain—

"Where you going, Tyler?"

Dez appeared so suddenly in front of him, that Tyler stumbled backward as if she'd pushed him.

Quick. Answer her.

"Hey, uh—hey, Dez. I'm, you know, stretching my legs a little."

He peered past her, looking for the big guy or the blue-eyed corpse man. They were nowhere to be seen. He released a jagged breath. That had to be a good sign. Little Dez wasn't going to rough him up.

Dez licked the corner of her mouth. "You need to settle up before you go. You know that, right?"

She clenched a fist and released it. In her sleeveless top, by the light of the streetlamp, Tyler saw the muscles in her arms bulge and relax.

Dez is ripped. How did I not notice that before?

"What?" He jerked back his neck, expression pinched as if she'd wounded him. "Of course I know I have to settle up—wait, you didn't think I was trying to sneak out, did you?" He laughed until Dez's stare made him feel like an idiot. His chuckles grew softer and farther between until they died.

Dez pulled something from her boot. Tyler didn't know what it was until she flicked her wrist and a small black, cylindrical object telescoped into a baton.

He put out both hands, palms up like he warding off evil spirits. "Whoa. Easy. You don't have to do anything like that."

"I'm afraid it's looking like I do," she said, sounding grim.

"Seriously? Look, yes, I *may* have played a little too deep tonight—"

"And last night."

"And last night. And *no*, I'll be honest with you—I don't have what I owe *on* me. But I signed a multi-million dollar deal. You know I'm good for it."

She took a step forward. "I don't know you at all."

He clapped his palms together in mea culpa. "Easy, Dez. Stop. Please. You can't mess me up. I'm due on set in a couple of days."

"Not my problem."

"Well, it kind of *is*. If I lose my part, I'll never get the money to pay you back."

Dez made a show of scratching her chin, pretending to be deep in thought.

"Nope. Still *your* problem."

He smiled to demonstrate he'd appreciated her little pantomime.

Everyone thinks they're an actor in Los Angeles.

A thought crossed his mind and he poked an index finger in her direction to punctuate his point. "The *studio*. Don't forget them. The studio will be *pissed* if you mess me up right before production starts."

Dez cocked her head. "Will they? Are you saying it'll be *hard* for them to find another fresh young face in Hollywood willing to play a superhero for millions of dollars?"

"I—" A different sort of fear washed through Tyler's nervous system. Dez and her baton weren't as scary as *other actors just like him.* What she'd said about his part—*that* was the thing of nightmares.

What if the studio replaces me?

Dez took another step forward.

Tyler felt panic rising in his chest. "Dez, look, we can work this out. I can get you the money. Next week—"

Dez's chin raised, ever so slightly.

For a second Tyler thought he'd captured her attention, but his relief proved short-lived.

She's not looking at me.

She was looking *past* him, over his shoulder.

Tyler heard the dirt crunch behind him.

Oh no.

Something struck the back of his skull.

He saw sparkles—like a burst of fireworks—and then, nothing.

Fiona watched as Dez and the large man with webs on his pudgy arms walked by carrying the boy, Tyler, between them. They humped him to a car, opened the trunk, and threw him inside.

Not so good at poker, that one.

The trunk slammed shut. Dez nodded to Fiona. Fiona nodded back.

Rune stood beside Fiona, sucking his canine tooth with his tongue.

"So you're saying it's that easy?" he asked, watching the car with Tyler inside roar away.

Fiona nodded. "Yep. I'm telling you. Take a walk around tomorrow. You'll *feel* the weakness. The desperation is almost choking. Everyone in this town is begging for someone to tempt them into something. *Anything.*"

"So, you're saying I should *stay* following my immediate business?"

"If you like. With the two of us here, anything is possible. Americans believe *everything* celebrities tell them. We influence the celebrities and they influence the country."

Rune grunted.

"Of course, there are two good guys here." She made air quotes with her fingers around the term *good guys*.

He turned to her. "Two. Plus that other girl?"

"The other girl?"

Rune shrugged and mumbled. "The one that looks like you."

"Catriona? You mean my sister?"

Rune grunted again.

Fiona sighed. "That's who I meant, Catriona and the Highlander."

Rune's mouth turned down. "Then there are *three*."

"Who's the third?"

"Ryft."

"Ryft?" Fiona repeated the name. She didn't know anyone named *Ryft*. She searched her memory for people she'd come in contact with, who'd given her the same feeling as Catriona and Broch.

No...I can't think of—

She gasped.

Sean.

It had to be. She'd rarely seen the man without Catriona or Broch nearby, so she'd attributed the odd tingling in the back of her neck to them.

"Is Ryft *Sean*? Sean Shaft? He works for Parasol. He's Catriona's adoptive father—"

A man walked by with a woman too attractive and tawdry to be his date. He threw a sloppy grin and winked at Rune, as if to say, *look what I got.*

Rune's lip snarled with apparent disgust, but he followed the man's progress until the drunk had disappeared around a corner.

Rune sniffed and turned back to Fiona.

"Ryft. What does he look like now?"

"Sean? He's older. Salt and pepper hair, close-cropped beard..."

Rune ran his left hand down his right arm to his glove. "It's *him.*"

"Who."

"The man who took my arm. The man who took *you.*"

She sighed. "Nobody took *me.*"

"When you were a baby here."

"I wasn't a baby *here.*"

"Yes, you were. I saved you from the breeding cow and then that man—"

"That was *Catriona.*" She shook her head. She'd hoped her father's time away had cured his mental irregularities, but it seemed he still had trouble telling her and her sister apart. He refused to admin Catriona existed, which, while adorable, could get annoying.

"We should probably get you home, dad."

Rune's expression flashed with anger. "What is this *dad.* Why do you call me that?"

"It's a name people call their fathers here."

"You may call me *Father.*"

She chuckled. "Okay. Whatever—"

He grabbed her upper arm with his gloved hand and Fiona knew it wasn't *flesh* filling that leather. His fingers felt harder and stronger than any human's. It was as if steel bands had wrapped around her bicep.

"You're *hurting* me." She tried to pull away but he held her easily.

Rune leaned his face to hers. His laser-like white eyes pointed through her brain.

"*Father,*" he repeated.

She nodded, frantic for him to release her. "Fine, yes. I'll call you Father. I'm sorry."

He let her go and she stepped away, rubbing at her arm.

"Show me Sean," he said.

She stared at the ground, anger burning in her chest. "I don't know where he is now. I'll take you to him tomorrow."

He glared at her, but she refused to be intimidated a second time.

"*Tomorrow,* Father. I have to sleep."

He sighed. "Fine. But know I'm disappointed."

He strode toward her car and stood at the passenger door, glaring back at her.

Pushing herself off the wall, Fiona followed. She'd *wanted* her father to find her.

She'd liked the idea of having an ally.

She'd forgotten about his temper, his moods, his breaks with reality...

Fiona clucked her tongue.

This might have been a mistake.

CHAPTER FOUR

Catriona entered Sean's office at nine-thirty a.m., already feeling behind schedule.

That morning, she'd been in the shower when the phone rang.

Rushing to get the shampoo out of her hair, she'd grabbed her cell on the fourth ring.

"Catriona?"

"Yes?" She'd glanced at her wet hand on the phone, wondering if she could be electrocuted by a cell.

"It's Bobby. I'm security at Studio Twelve. You told me to give you a call if I ever saw the big dude doing anything weird."

She'd groaned, dreading to hear what Broch had gotten himself into.

"He's at Studio Twelve? What's that? *Morning Chat*?"

"Yep."

"What's he doing?"

"Uh...he's *on air*."

"He's *what*?" Her screech made the shower door quiver.

She'd hung up the phone, thrown on jeans and a shirt that should have been tucked in but wouldn't be, skipped the elevator, and taken the stairs two flights to the payroll office beneath her apartment. She'd run past desk-bound Anne and bolted across the lot to Studio Twelve.

That's where, with wet hair and no makeup, she'd pulled Kilty away from the microphone. She hadn't even had a chance to yell at him when her phone rang a second time and Sean demanded they come to his office.

Weren't Fridays supposed to be easy days?

Now in Sean's office, she flopped to her seat beside Luther

on Sean's worn sofa. Her father's friend and work partner sat in his favorite corner, hidden behind his morning paper.

"Good morning, girlie," he said in his Barry White baritone.

"Good morning, Luther." She threw her head back to stare at the ceiling. Broch wandered in. He'd fallen behind when the laces on his leather boots came untied. She thought the soft boots looked as if he'd made them himself out of roadkill, and since they'd come with him via old-timey Scotland, she probably wasn't far off.

"What's wrong with you?" asked Sean, blithely enjoying his morning coffee like a person *not* in charge of wrangling rogue Highlanders.

Catriona sighed. "I remember that."

"What?"

"Enjoying a cup of coffee in the morning. Must be nice."

Sean smiled at Broch as his son took a seat in the chair across from his desk. As usual, the Highlander looked happy as a puppy.

Catriona scowled. "*I* didn't have the luxury of a cup of coffee this morning."

Sean took a sip from his mug. "Should I guess from the way you're staring laser holes through the side of Broch's head, that your lack of caffeine has something to do with *him*?"

"You *should*. I got a call from Bobby, security over at *Morning Chat*. It seems some kilted idiot wandered to the question mic seeking love advice this morning.

Luther snorted a laugh. Catriona tried to throw her disapproval in his direction, but he shifted his paper to block her view.

Sean peered down his nose at Broch. "You were on set? During filming?"

Broch held out his hands and tilted his palms to the ceiling.

"The woman's man cuidnae fin' a place tae hing his towel, sae ah tellt her aboot the hook oan the back o' the door, 'n' then thay asked me if ah had quaistions."

Sean turned back to Catriona. "You're sure he was on the air?"

She nodded. "Yep. As was I. No makeup, wet hair...generally looking like a crazy person because *I didn't get my coffee*."

Sean rubbed his temple. "You can't go on sets, son. Not when they're filming."

"Sorry." Broch nodded and stood to pour himself a cup of coffee from Sean's machine. "Ah should tell ye, thare wis a wifie thare wha touched mah hindquarters. Ah think that's against policy."

Sean glanced at Catriona, his expression hovering somewhere between alarmed and amused. She shrugged, flopping her hands to her sides. "I have no idea what he's talking about."

Catriona watched as Broch poured the last drop of coffee from the carafe into his mug and settled back into his chair to enjoy it.

"You're lucky I wouldn't drink that coffee on a bet," she grumbled.

Sean glanced in his mug. "There's nothing wrong with my coffee."

Catriona scoffed and tried to fluff her hair in the hopes it might dry *pretty*.

"So what did you need?" she asked Sean.

"I need you to check on Tyler Bash. I'm hearing rumors he got into some trouble last night and he's not answering his phone."

"What kind of trouble?"

"Celebrity poker game. He lost, and I don't think it's the first time. Sounds like someone tried to collect and he made a run for it."

"One of Alain's games?"

Sean nodded.

A small-time French gangster known as Little Alain ran the largest and most prestigious underground celebrity poker game in Hollywood. No one called him Little Alain to his face, though. Five-foot-five of pure Napoleon complex, Alain had dealt broken bones, missing teeth, and missed call times to Parasol Pictures talent in the past. He didn't mess around.

Sean handed Catriona a slip of paper. "Here's the address Tyler was playing at last night. See if you can find any cameras. Check his house first. I added his address there, too."

She stood and took the torn notebook page. "You know, you could *text* me this stuff."

Sean shrugged. "Why, when I have a perfectly good pen here?"

Broch threw back the last of his swill and stood to put the cup back near the machine.

"You stay out of the studios," said Sean, following his movements.

Broch offered a sheepish smile. "Aye."

Catriona reached for the door and heard Sean whisper behind her. "And keep an eye on her."

"Aye."

She turned. "Kilty's not my *bodyguard*. I did this job *fine* before he dropped out of the sky."

Broch scratched his head. "Ah don't think ah fell oot o' the sky."

She pointed at him. "You shut it. You're on my last nerve today."

He tucked back his neck to keep her finger from poking him in the chin. "Ye wouldnae be sae cranky if ye'd juist marry me. Ah—" He sent a sideward glance in Sean's direction before lowering his voice to a whisper to her. "Ah cuid explain why later."

Luther snickered from behind his paper.

Catriona huffed. "Don't encourage him." She flung open the door and hustled from the office, striding down the hall until she reached outside.

Broch followed on her heels. "Whaur ur we gaun?"

She glanced up at him as he flanked her. "Let's get a few things straight—"

Broch rolled his eyes. "Och, here we gae."

"First off, I've told you a million times *do not go on sets without me.*"

He nodded. "Sorry. Ah watch they wummin oan mah television set 'n' ah couldnae hulp myself."

The way Broch said the word *television* with no Scottish accent made it hard for Catriona not to laugh. It sounded like a bad dubbing, where a different actor had filled in the word. It was how he pronounced all words unfamiliar to his eighteenth-century Scottish vocabulary and it never ceased to amuse her. But giggling in the middle of a scolding would sap all the power from it, so she set her jaw and continued.

"You could cost Parasol thousands if they have to reshoot a scene because you wandered through some modern-day romantic comedy in that filthy kilt."

He loured at her. "'Tisn't *filthy*. Ye washed it and erased a decade o' fine seasoning, remember?"

She ignored him. "Second, don't ever tell me I won't be

cranky if I marry you."

He chuckled. "Did ye understand whit ah wis sayin'? Ah wis sayin' wance ye slipped intae mah kip, I'd—"

She held up a hand to stop him. "Yeah, I got it. The point is, you said you'd *pound the cranky out of me* in front of my *father*."

"Ah didnae say *pound*." He smirked. "Though 'tis fair 'n' accurate."

"You *implied* it in front of Sean."

"Sae?"

"*Sae* you may be his real son but he *raised* me. What if some guy came to your crappy mud hut—or whatever hovel you lived in back in *Outlander*-land—looking for your *daughter*? Said he was hoping to work the temper out of her?"

Broch's expression clouded. "Ah'd knock his head aff his neck."

"*Exactly*. Sean doesn't want to think about me in anyone's *kip*. And he's not stupid, he knows there's something between us, but the whole thing puts him in a weird position, worrying we'll be hurt and he'll have to take sides."

"Whyfur wid we git hurt?"

Catriona sighed. "Things happen. Believe me."

Broch slapped a hand to his chest. "Dae ye think Sean wouldn't give his blessing tae me?"

"It isn't that. I'm sure he's proud of the big slab of haggis you've grown into. But we're both his kids."

Broch recoiled. "Nae we aren't."

"Not by *blood*, but it's still a lot to deal with. So no sex talk in front of Sean, okay?"

He nodded. "Ah ken."

Catriona realized her directions had been too specific. "Wait, what I mean is, no sex talk in front of anyone, *especially* Sean."

"Aye."

She took a moment to gather her thoughts.

I know there was a third thing...

"Oh, and last, don't you *ever* tell me a little time in your kip would change my attitude. It's insulting."

He giggled. "Aye?"

The sound of his child-like amusement made her laugh. "*Yes*. It makes it sound like women's brains don't work without a man."

Broch tilted his head. "Ye said it..."

Amy Vansant

She punched him in the side of his pec.

"Ow."

He grabbed his chest, giggling harder.

CHAPTER FIVE

Catriona pulled as close as she could to Tyler Bash's house in the Hollywood hills, parking her Jeep on the steep street outside. She put the vehicle in park and looked at Broch, who sat in the passenger seat, still in his kilt.

"Let me do the talking," she said, opening her door.

He scoffed. "Lik' ah cuid stop ye."

Trudging up the hill, they navigated to the gate at the end of Tyler's driveway. Catriona pressed the button on the callbox several times. No one answered.

"We really should look inside," she said, tilting back her head to eyeball the tall gate.

Without another word, Broch jumped, grabbing the top horizontal bar of the gate and hoisting himself up with one mighty pull-up. Swinging a leg over the spiked top of the gate with more grace than Catriona would have imagined possible in a large man wearing a skirt, he balanced there, stabilizing his position. As his other leg arced, she caught a flash of neon yellow. It seemed his love affair with the boxer briefs she'd bought him hadn't ended.

Thank you, Calvin Klein.

At least she didn't have to worry about him flashing the family jewels with every twirl of his tartan.

Broch held himself suspended on the opposite side of the gate and reached down toward her.

"Ah'll hoist ye up."

She shook her head. "Uh-uh. Drop down and hit the button on the box on the other side."

He fell to his leather-booted feet and found the control panel. The doors cranked open and Catriona walked inside like a civilized human being.

"Let's get a move on before the neighbors call the cops about a monkey wearing a skirt." She reached under his kilt, and sliding her fingers beneath the thin fabric of his boxer briefs, gave them a playful snap.

He spun away from her. "Hey, *harassment.* That's workplace harassment, lassie. Ah learnt aboot it and ah'll report ye."

She chuckled. "I wish all the new employees took that course to heart the way you did."

Striding up the driveway to the house, Catriona let her gaze wander, searching for anything odd on the grounds. All seemed well until they reached the cement porch of the Spanish-style home.

The ornately carved front door was ajar.

Not a good sign.

No telling what waited inside. She patted her hip and glanced back in the direction of the Jeep.

I should have brought my gun.

She motioned for Broch to step away from the direct line of the door and pushed it open with her fingertips.

"Hello? Tyler?"

Nothing.

She poked her head inside.

The place was a mess.

Like many young stars, Tyler had the money for a fancy house but not the taste or brains to hire a decorator. The inside looked as if a college student had moved into a deserted mansion. A worn black leather sofa demanded center stage. The coffee table—an early-American-style hand-me-down from *mom*, no doubt—served as support for a video game machine and its corresponding controllers. The side table, fashioned from a whiskey barrel, sported a lamp made from a whiskey bottle.

At least that part of the room has a theme.

They wandered through the rooms finding varying degrees of mess, but little evidence as to what had happened to Tyler.

"Whit now?" asked Broch, plucking an apple from a bowl on the counter and biting into it.

Catriona sighed. "Well, we can find out who saw him—"

"Who are you?"

A blonde appeared in the living room, staring at Catriona, a paper grocery bag tucked in the crook of her arm.

Catriona detected a nervous lilt lacing the girl's inquiry.

"We work for Parasol. Who are you?"

Broch moved behind Catriona and the girl's shoulders released. Catriona could tell by the girl's reaction she'd been relieved to see Broch.

Ah.

She'd been worried Catriona was *competition* for Tyler's affections.

"I'm Tyler's girlfriend, Abigail," she said, confirming Catriona's suspicion.

Abigail had every right to be worried. She was smack in the middle of one of Hollywood's oldest stories. The hometown girlfriend comes to L.A. with the movie star wannabe—he gets the big check and she gets the boot.

Catriona leaned forward to shake the girl's hand. "Nice to meet you. Do you know where we can find Tyler?"

The girl puffed a clump of hair from where it had flopped over one eye and placed her groceries on the counter.

"He didn't come home last night."

"Do you know where he went?"

"To get his fix."

"Drugs?"

Abigail chuckled without mirth. "Worse. Poker."

"Alain's game?"

"Who?"

"Did he mention a Frenchman?"

The girl nodded, her consideration rolling to Broch as he took another loud bite of apple.

"You're enormous. Are you an actor?"

Broch shook his head. "Na."

"So it was the Frenchman's game?" repeated Catriona, hoping to hold Abigail's attention for more than ten seconds. Talking to people even seven years younger than her sometimes felt like trying to catch a drunken moth in a jar.

The girl pulled a quart of coconut milk and a box of bean sprouts from her bag and motioned for Broch to step aside so she could open the refrigerator. "Yes. He said it was the Frenchman's game the first time he went, the day before. He was super excited to be invited."

"And you haven't heard from him since he left for last night's game?"

She shook her head.

"Okay. Thank you. If you hear from him, give the studio a call or have him call. We need him to check-in."

Abigail nodded.

Catriona motioned to Broch. "Let's go."

Broch popped the last bit of apple in his mouth and crunched on the core as he smiled at the girl. "Nice tae meet ye."

The girl nodded, her mouth downturned. Catriona didn't get the feeling she liked her new home in L.A., but the coconut milk and sprouts implied she was *trying* to adapt.

Catriona and Broch made their way back to the gate. On the way, she called Robert Williams. Last she'd heard, the old movie star still liked his cards.

"Hello, Robert Williams here, how can I help you?" At seventy-two, the actor's voice still poured like melted caramel through the phone.

"You still playing in the Frenchman's game?"

Robert chuckled. "Still winning so I'm still playing."

Catriona could almost *hear* him grinning with pride. "Did you see fresh meat last night by the name of Tyler Bash?"

Robert chuckled. "The *freshest*. He'd come before but he opened his veins last night."

"How'd that end?"

"You know, I don't know. He was behind. Left to go to the john I think. That was the last I saw of him."

"You notice anyone go after him?"

"No. But I had my head in the game. That's why I don't lose."

"Where was the game last night?"

"Jay's place. The room over the bar."

"Okay. That's all I need. Thanks, Bob."

"No problem gorgeous. Tell your rascal of a father I miss him at the games."

"Will do."

Catriona hung up. Most of the old guard at Parasol had massive respect for Sean, and by association, for her. It was nice to have the wisdom of the studio at her fingertips when she needed it.

"Where noo?" asked Broch as they hopped in the Jeep.

"The Frenchman, Alain, runs a poker game for celebrities. Someone as new as Tyler only gets invited for one reason—to be bled dry. They knew he'd lose it."

"Ye think he coudnae pay his debts?"

She nodded. "And Alain's been known to get creative when actors can't pay."

Catriona drove them to Jay's Joint, a popular West Hollywood spot for celebrities to hide. Pulling to the curb, she scanned the outside of the building. Cameras hung outside, but she knew she wouldn't get footage from Jay without a fight. The privacy of his clientele was too precious.

She could call Sean in to pull some strings or...

She twisted for a new view. Across the street, she spotted another camera mounted on the front of a coffee shop. Instead of pointing at the entrance of the shop, it glared directly at the front of Jay's.

Ha. Gotcha.

A girl and a guy stood behind the counter inside the coffee shop.

Baristas.

She poked Broch on the arm.

"Come with me. I might need you."

Broch stretched his back. "Whatfur?"

"There's a young man and woman behind the counter of that coffee shop across the street. Between the two of us, we should be able to charm *someone* into giving me what I want."

She didn't add that, in West Hollywood, the odds were better that he'd come in handy for the boy.

They entered the shop to the happy ringing of a bell. The girl didn't bother to look up from her phone. The young man stopped wiping the counter, seemingly mesmerized by Broch.

Bingo.

"How can I help *you*?"

Catriona elbowed Broch in his side. "Introduce yourself."

Broch flinched. "Huh? Och, ah'm Broch." He leaned forward and thrust his hand across the counter.

"I'm Brian. We're both B's." Instead of shaking Broch's hand he curled his fingers against the inside of Broch's digits to create a c-shaped chain link. "I love your kilt."

Broch beamed. "Thank ye. Thank ye fer nae callin' it a skirt." He shot Catriona a look, coming just short of sticking out his tongue.

Spotlight on her, Catriona stepped up. "Brian, I was wondering if you could help us. I—I mean, *we*—need to see last night's footage from that camera you have out there. Could we take a peek at that?"

Brian glanced at her, seemingly annoyed to find her present. "Can't do that."

"Not even for Broch?"

Broch grinned.

Brian melted for a moment and then resumed his annoyed snarl at Catriona.

"Are you a cop?"

Catriona shook her head.

"Then *no*. Not allowed to." His gaze swiveled back to Broch and then softened again. "I wish I could, but the owner wouldn't like it. I'd lose my job. You understand."

"Aye."

Brian giggled. "Where are you from with that accent?"

Catriona sighed.

So much for charm. Time for blackmail.

She pushed in front of Broch. "So, would your refusal be because the *owner* is selling the footage of Jay's to the tabloid shows, or because *you* are selling it and you're afraid he'll find out?"

Brian paled. "I'm sure I don't know what you mean."

His co-worker snorted a laugh. Catriona glanced at her, but she dropped her attention back to her phone as if pulled by a magnet.

Catriona smiled. The girl knew it was Brian's scheme.

Got ya.

"Gosh, Brian, are you *sure* you don't know what I mean? I can explain it to you." Catriona pointed outside. "The camera out there isn't directed at your door. It's pointed across the street at Jay's. Lots of interesting people go in and out of Jay's, don't you think?"

Brian's eyes darted in the direction of his co-worker as he leaned forward, his voice dropping to a whisper. "If the boss finds out, I'm fired."

"So let me look at the recording. I'm not going to say anything."

Brian sighed and caught Broch's eye. "Is she always this tough?"

Broch smiled. "Ye hae nae idea."

Brian motioned for them to come around the counter and led them through a curtain to a back office.

He pulled a VHS tape from a backpack, looking sheepish.

"You're not going to take it, are you?"

Probably.

Catriona shook her head. "No. It's an actual tape? It isn't digital?"

Brian rolled his eyes. "Greg is cheap. This system's like a thousand years old."

"Greg's the owner?"

"Uh-huh."

"And this is the only copy? You were taking it home?"

He nodded and grinned as if he couldn't help himself. "It's a *good* one."

Brian slipped the tape into the machine and rewound it for a few seconds. Catriona stared at an empty street illuminated by street lamps until a man and a woman appeared at the entrance to the alley beside Jay's. Between them, they carried the seemingly unconscious body of a young blond man.

"That's Tyler," said Broch, pointing.

"What's wrong with him?" asked Catriona to no one in particular.

Brian shrugged. "I don't know how he got like that, but here comes the interesting part."

The woman and the man put Tyler in the trunk of a black Mercedes sedan. They spoke for a moment before the man lumbered back inside Jay's and the woman drove the Mercedes out of view.

Brian reached to stop the tape just as another man and a woman walked out of the building.

Catriona touched his arm. "Wait."

The couple stood outside Jay's talking. The man was impossibly thin. The woman was all too familiar.

"Is that Fiona?" asked Broch, leaning in to get a better look. He glanced at Catriona. "And yer da?"

Catriona didn't answer. She couldn't. She felt as though someone had flash-frozen her insides. The nerves in her arms jangled with what could only be described as *dread*.

Since her father had arrived in town, she'd been trying to pretend he *hadn't*. Seeing him moving and breathing made her plan more difficult.

She remained transfixed by the screen until the two figures walked out of frame, first her father, followed by her sister.

"What are *they* doing there?" she mumbled under her breath. Worry buzzed in the back of her brain like a fly trapped under glass.

Fiona had told her their father was a man to be feared—that he'd killed their mother and tried to kill her.

She didn't remember that.

Broch knew Rune as the man who shot her dead in another life. At first, Catriona *thought* she'd met Broch for the first time when he appeared on the studio lot, but *no*. It turned out she'd once died in his arms, shot dead by her own father.

She didn't remember that either.

Maybe that was a good thing.

After that, according to the story Sean and Broch pieced together slowly and over much whiskey, she went spinning through time, appearing reborn in, well, *now*. Sean adopted her as a child, coming to know Rune as the man who'd killed her new, modern-day L.A. mother. And for some reason, neither Sean nor Broch could explain, Rune had a habit of calling her by her sister's name, *Fiona*. Which was odd, but possibly less disturbing than the realization that Rune had killed *both* the mothers she didn't remember.

Catriona cocked her head.

It certainly doesn't pay to be my mother.

It didn't pay to be her father either. Sean had cleft Rune nearly in two while saving her from his clutches. This triggered the apparent reason for her family's time-traveling abilities—some sort of preservation mechanism that swapped certain death for life in another century. Sean's attack sent Rune off to god-knows-where.

Death, or near-death, *had* to be the cause for all the time-traveling. She'd been sent to the future after being shot, Sean had been run through by a sword, Broch had been stabbed...

Not only were her family and friends time travelers, but they were also accident-prone death magnets.

Anyway, now Rune was back.

Yea.

He'd survived Sean's attack—though when she saw him, his arm looked suspicious, his hand gloved. She suspected his limb may *not* have survived. Broch still had a scar where Fiona had stabbed him, so remnants of "mortal" wounds seemed to stick around if they were wounds inflicted by other time travelers.

Hm.

"Do you need to see it again?" asked Brian.

Catriona snapped to the present.

"Huh?"

Wow. I am doing a great *job not thinking about my psycho father.*

"Do you need to see the tape again?"

"Oh. No."

Catriona pushed the eject button and retrieved the tape before nudging Broch. "Let's go."

Brian's eyes popped wide. "Hey, wait, you can't take the tape."

"Oh, but I'm going to."

Brian gasped. "But you said you wouldn't!"

"I lied."

Brian lunged for the tape but Catriona easily jerked it from his reach. Broch stepped between them, staring down at the barista.

"Na."

Brian swallowed and crossed his arms over his chest. "Bitch."

Broch's neck cricked down to pull his face closer to Brian's. "Ye call her that again and ah'll tie ye intae a breid knot yer partner can sell to the next man wha rings the bell."

With a bravery Catriona hadn't suspected in the boy, Brian lifted his chin to stare back into Broch's eyes.

"I wasn't talking about *her.*"

Broch's brow knit and Catriona tugged him through the curtain, through the shop, and back onto the street. The girl never looked up from her phone as they left the store.

They were in the Jeep when Broch cocked his head to the side. "That Brian reminded me o' a strange laddie ah knew wance..."

Catriona started the truck. "Back in your time it was probably dangerous for men to be like Brian, but it isn't like that now." She paused. "At least it isn't supposed to be. Some people still aren't nice."

Broch shrugged. "The boy ah ken wis an odd but good lad. Made me a fine cloak once, fer nae reason, and gave it tae me—" Broch turned to her, his expression wide.

Catriona smirked. "What?"

"Och. Ah juist realized how come he gave me the cloak."

Catriona laughed.

CHAPTER SIX

Tyler's eyes fluttered open.

I'm dead.

He surveyed the largest room he'd ever seen. Things memories tricked forward. His brain felt like it was made out of wet socks.

Wall. Glass. Light. Sofa.

Tilting back his head, he squinted at the lights above him. The ceiling had to be thirty feet high. One entire wall was glass, but from his vantage, he could only see the sky and the very corner of what he assumed was another building.

My shoulders hurt.

He tried to move his arms but found them pinned behind him. Looking down, he traced the edges of the object beneath his butt.

A chair. I'm tied to a chair in a palace...am I on set?

He scanned the room for a camera and a crew. Maybe he was filming a movie and he'd blacked out—

"Look who's awake."

A girl with latte-colored skin walked in, her hips twitching inside tight black leather pants. As she shut the door behind her, Tyler caught a flash of what looked like a hotel hallway.

Front door.

He realized he'd missed the chance to scream for help.

The girl came into focus once more.

I know her.

Dez.

Dez had been in the alley.

The poker game...

He swallowed. "Where am I?"

Without answering, Dez strode across the room. He stretched his neck to watch her place a plastic bag on a marble island behind him. His bound wrists kept him from seeing much more.

Something moved in the main room and Tyler turned forward again. A man strolled through an archway across from Tyler, fifty feet from where he sat. This new man sported slicked steel-gray hair and wore a cream-colored suit, lending more credence to Tyler's first theory—that he'd died and gone to heaven.

Did I—? No.

His bound hands and the presence of Dez blew sizeable holes in any *heaven* hypothesis.

The man didn't look like God, either. At least none Tyler had ever imagined. He was small, with a nose a little too large for his face. He wore a large gold and diamond ring on his wedding finger.

God wouldn't be married, would he?

Tyler couldn't tell if the man was happy...*maybe amused?* The corner of his mouth curled in a permanent smirk.

The cat who ate the canary.

That's what his mother would call the man's expression.

Tyler sighed.

I'd love to be at home with Mom right now.

Mini-god nodded at a plump chair covered in gold and cream cloth. Dez appeared from behind Tyler to move the chair into position, parking it in front of him.

The man sauntered to the chair and sat facing him. He crossed his legs and picked at one of his fingernails with his thumb.

Tyler couldn't take the silence any longer. "Who are you?"

The man looked up from his nails. "You dahn't know me?"

He shook his head. *Was that an accent?*

The little man sniffed. "Should I be offended? After all, you have one hundred and sirty-seven dollars of my money."

Oh.

Now Tyler knew he wasn't in heaven. He was being punished for not paying his gambling debts.

That made more sense.

"You're the Frenchman?"

Alain shrugged one shoulder. "You can call me zat. Many do. Or you can call me Alain."

Tyler nodded and tried to keep from crying by thinking positive thoughts, like all the self-motivation books he'd read told him to do in situations like this.

Well, not *exactly* like this.

Alain seems reasonable. The French are super civil, right?

"You invented democracy, right?"

Tyler didn't mean to ask the question out loud, but thanks to high school history, it was the only thing he knew about the French and the words had tumbled from his mouth like he was taking an oral exam.

Alain squinted at him and then scowled at Dez. "Why ees 'e talking about democracy and not my money?"

Dez shrugged. "You know us Americans. We're all crazy for democracy."

Tyler tried to get his thoughts in order, but his mind kept drifting to his arms. His shoulders *burned*.

"Mr. Alain, I want you to know I'm going to get you your money. Every cent."

Alain nodded. "I know you are."

"Right. So, I guess what I'm saying is, *message received.* Loud and clear. You didn't have to do this. I wouldn't have *not* paid you."

"I know this too."

Tyler nodded. "Right. Good. So we understand each other?"

Alain crossed his hands on his knee. "You are new to ze games. I do not know you. Ziss ees necessary so that you know *me*. You understand?"

Tyler laughed, his nerves pushing what he'd thought was a chuckle into an ear-shattering *guffaw*. "*Absolutely*. You can't let any old slacker lose money and think they're going to walk away."

"Exactly. I'm glad we are on ze same page."

"Me too. So, I'll find my way back. No problem. I have to be on set Monday. I'll have your money to you by Friday—"

Alain clucked his tongue. "Friday? Oh no. I don't sink you want to wait until Friday."

"I need to—" Tyler stopped, his brow knitting. Something about the way Alain said that last bit didn't feel right. "Wait. Why?"

"Eet's a lot of words."

"Wads?"

"*Words.*"

"Words?"

Alain nodded. "Oui." He looked to Dez, who emptied a plastic bag onto the counter as if he'd asked her to do it. Tyler heard metal clanking. Dez rustled around somewhere behind him for several seconds before walking into view holding what looked like a metal X-Acto knife. His mother used one very much like it for crafting back in Wisconsin.

Boy, do I miss Wisconsin.

The knife had a razor-sharp, pointed blade at one end, and a metal, pencil-sized body.

Tyler eyeballed Dez in her leather pants. She didn't look like the *crafting* sort.

"What's that for?"

"Eet's how she's going to write ze words on your body."

"On my *body*?"

"Oui. We start with the thigh, no? No one will see that in your modest American swimming trunks. But next, we move to your—what do you sink? Stomach? Back? Forehead?"

Tyler shook his head. "Whoa, wait, you can't cut my face—I'm an *actor*—My face is my *life*." Even in his rising panic, Tyler knew it was the *douchiest* thing he'd ever said in his life.

"Zen maybe you pay me een two days and we spare ze face?"

Tyler's head began to buzz with a high-pitched wail he couldn't identify.

Am I making that whine? Or does fear have a sound?

"How can I get you money tied to a chair?"

Alain shrugged. "I will let you make some phone calls."

"*Phone calls?* Who am I going to call? My parents don't have that kind of money. I...I..."

Tyler found it hard to breathe. Spittle flew from his lips as he stammered, searching for the words to pull him from his nightmare.

"I'll pay, but I need—"

"What do you sink we should write first?"

Alain acted as if Tyler wasn't writhing in front of him. Tyler sobbed so hard he saw tears shoot from his face as if his eyes were little cannons. If he wasn't so panicked, he'd think it was funny.

Alain didn't respond to panic.

He had to calm down.

Baseball. Sure, think about baseball. Breathe. Think about the

Brewers...ohmygod I'm going to die...

Alain looked at Dez, searching for an answer. "What do you sink?"

Dez put a finger to her chin in a cartoonish gesture of deep thought. "Hm. That's a good question. We could carve *cheater*?"

Tyler nearly fainted. Why did she have to say *carve*?

Alain shook his head. "No, I don't seenk so. Zat would imply he cheated at cards, don't you sink? He didn't cheat, or he'd already be dead."

Dez laughed. "True. Welcher?"

Alain pointed at her. "Zat's a good one."

Tyler jerked forward, straining against his bonds. "Are you people *insane*? You can't carve words into me. I'm a star!"

Alain didn't look at him. "How about *I don't pay my debts*?"

Tyler did his best to speak through his racking sobs, words spitting in staccato bursts. "That's a... freaking... sentence... that's four words...no, *five*—"

Alain faced him. "At least I used a contraction for *do not*, or eet would be six."

"Ooh, how about *deadbeat*?" offered Dez.

Tyler's attention whipped to the woman holding the craft knife. "Stop sounding so *excited*. Stop it. Both of you, I get it. You made your point."

Alain nodded. "Oui. I like that best. *Deadbeat* it is."

Dez raised the blade. "The thigh?"

"Oui."

Tyler shook his head so hard the chair rocked. "No, no, no, no. *Bum*. What about *bum*? *Bum's* a good word."

Dez pushed up the left leg of his shorts and he wailed like a siren, unable to stop.

"I didn't get my phone call!"

CHAPTER SEVEN

So many chances.

No more.

No more coddling.

Rune could remember the first time he realized his very presence improved the people around him.

Somewhere around 900 A.D. in what was now Norway. He'd inspired a thief to return a cloth-wrapped package of salted fish to a vendor. It hadn't been difficult, and that first time, it made him feel good.

The feeling didn't last.

He remembered one inferior person after the next *thriving* thanks to his strange ability to offer them hope, courage, patience, inspiration...whatever it was they needed.

After watching undeserving men and women misuse their newfound inner fortitude, he realized the awful truth.

People didn't deserve his help.

He was throwing off the natural order.

In 1864, Herbert Spencer first used the phrase *survival of the fittest.*

Rune liked the theory.

Of course, Charles Darwin, quoting Spencer five years later in *On the Origin of the Species*, would get credit for the phrase in history. In that case, it was *survival of the more widely published.*

History only remembered the winners. Many of them horrible people, in truth. Some of which, he'd given a leg up.

Not any more.

He stared at Parasol Pictures' front gate, tapping on the steering wheel of Fiona's Lexus with his index finger.

Come out, come out, wherever you are.

Rune realized the truth behind *survival of the fittest* long before Spencer or Darwin's grandparents were even born. Survival of the fittest became a religion for him, and his faith was strong enough to change his very being. Weak people began to grow *weaker* around him. He found he could tempt muddle-minded fools into *anything*. A few choice words in the their ear...very few had the moral and mental fortitude to withstand a pull toward an easier path.

Very few.

He was like the Wizard of Oz if the Wizard had given the Scarecrow a brain so he could use it to build a nuclear bomb.

Idiots. All of them.

Rune found his calling. Using their weakness against them, he rid the world of stupid, vicious vermin.

But his plans progressed slowly. He was only one man, and he'd suffered setbacks of his own.

First, his daughter rebelled and ran away.

Then Ryft nearly cut him in half. He had to be born anew. Had to grow up all over again.

He looked down at the gloved hand resting in his lap and sent impulses from his brain to the circuitry to wiggle his metal fingers.

Born without an arm.

Now he was back and Fiona seemed willing to rejoin him in his quest. The world could be controlled through a computer screen or phone. Together, they could find a hundred ways to amplify their influence. Hollywood...social media...all they had to do was inspire the right people and the world would collapse on itself.

Only the strongest would survive.

Survival of the fittest.

Rune caught movement through his windshield and looked up to watch a bearded man wave at a security guard as he walked through the gate and out of the Parasol Pictures lot, headed for his car.

Ryft.

Rune pressed the ignition button and shifted into drive.

CHAPTER EIGHT

Catriona tossed the VHS tape on Sean's desk with a clattering of plastic.

"What's this?"

"It's a video of an unconscious Tyler Bash being thrown into the trunk of a black Mercedes and driven away."

Sean cocked an eyebrow. "Please tell me this is some kind of new actor prank."

She shook her head. "No such luck. It happened outside Jay's last night. I don't know the guy carrying him on his shoulders, but the girl is Dez."

"Alain's Dez?"

"Yep. Tyler's girlfriend confirmed he has gambling issues. He left to play and never came home. Robert Williams says Tyler was at the game and he was losing."

Sean chuckled. "Bob Williams. That old fox is still playing, huh?"

"He said to say *hi*."

"Hm." Sean sighed. "So the kid owes Alain money. You've run into Dez before?"

"Once or twice."

"Careful. That little girl packs a punch. I once watched her beat a man twice her size unconscious."

"You didn't stop her?"

Sean shrugged. "He didn't work for us and her bloodlust faded pretty quickly with me nearby."

It took Catriona a moment before she realized what Sean was telling her. "You influenced Dez to be a better person? Just by being there?"

He nodded. "Though it works better if you concentrate on

it."

"Hm. I'll have to give that a shot."

Sean rocked in his chair. "We need Tyler back by Monday or this is going to be a real problem. I'll call Alain. In the meantime, you two pack for Vegas. Even if I convince Alain to let him go, he isn't going to deliver him."

"You think he took the kid to Las Vegas?"

"More than likely. That's his home base."

Sean grabbed his phone and Catriona turned to leave.

"Where's Broch?" asked Sean as he searched for the number to dial.

Catriona opened the door.

"I left him talking to half a horse."

Sean nodded. "Tell him not to lend him any money. Go pack."

Catriona stepped outside to find Broch pulling a twenty-dollar bill out of the leather sporran she liked to call his man-purse.

She hastened forward and caught his hand before he could pass the money to a man leaning against the wall of Studio Three, smoking a cigar. The man wore the back-end of a sparkling pink pony costume.

"Rick needs money," said Broch.

"No. Rick knows because he works on a kid show, people don't immediately realize what an asshole he is." She scowled at the half-man, half-pony. "Shame on you. Quit taking advantage of the new employees."

Rick frowned. "You're no fun."

Catriona motioned to the cigar. "And you know Gustav hates the smell of those things."

Gustav was the magical pony's *head*.

Rick rolled his eyes and muttered a profanity to show how little he cared about the preferences of his better half.

Catriona tapped Broch's arm. "Come on. We have to pack for Vegas."

Broch shrugged at Rick and followed Catriona away.

"Rick said his hoose burned down," he said as they headed for their apartments above the payroll office.

"He lied."

"He said he lost everything."

"He lied twice. If you'd given him that twenty, next week his parakeet will have contracted bird flu and he'll need money for the vet."

"Whit's Vegas?"

"I'm not sure I can explain Vegas to you. You sort of have to see it."

"Try."

Catriona hooked a thumb back toward Rick. "Picture that guy, the one wearing half a sparkling pink pony costume, as the most *normal* person here."

Broch frowned. "Whit?"

"Picture the Parasol studio lot, only everything is three times as big, three times as weird, and covered with lights, boobs and glitter."

Broch frowned.

"Ah cannae. Yer tairible at this."

Catriona shrugged. "It's not my fault. I told you you wouldn't be able to picture it. You'll understand when we get there."

The phone in Catriona's pocket dinged and she retrieved it to find a new text message from Sean.

Can't reach Alain but you'll find him at the penthouse of the golden tower.

"The *golden tower*?" She winced. "That's a *terrible* name."

Her phone dinged again.

Get a blank check from Jeanie. Tell her I okayed it.

He didn't know Jeanie was on vacation. No matter. That wasn't the important part.

Catriona grinned.

Loose in Vegas with a blank check?

"We're going shopping," she said aloud.

"We are?"

"No. Just kidding. Joke to myself."

"Och. Hilarious. Be sure tae shaur yer next private joke wi' me tae."

She glanced at him. "You know, you've gotten a lot more sarcastic since you showed up here."

Broch muttered under his breath. "Ah wonder how come."

Her phone dinged again.

Take the jet.

"Really? This is like Christmas. We get to take the jet."

Broch paled. "Ah don't lik' planes."

"It beats driving four hours."

"Nae it doesnae."

They entered the payroll office and Catriona smiled as she approached Anne. The substitute payroll clerk sat behind her desk in a turquoise scoop-neck tee looking even more like an ex-model than she had the last time she saw her.

Why the redhead was working in a payroll office and not making *bank* on her good looks, she didn't know.

Anne smiled. "Hello. How are you two today?"

Broch nodded his head in Catriona's direction. "She willnae marry me."

Anne blinked at him.

"Uhhh…"

Catriona rolled her eyes. "We're fine. I need a check." Anne didn't need to know Broch thought they needed to be married to protect *her* honor. His logic didn't even make sense unless Anne *also* knew he'd been born in the seventeen hundreds, and the poor woman didn't need to know *that*.

"A *check*—?"

"Yep. An actual check. *Blank.* I need to give an actor a temporary loan. They're in the black book in that drawer there." Catriona pointed to the drawer. She knew where the checks were. She'd borrowed a few in the past.

She held up her phone so Anne could see Sean's message, but the redhead didn't seem to care. She opened the drawer, pulled out an oversized checkbook, and detached one.

"Here you go. Where are you going?" asked Anne, handing it over.

Broch's expression clouded. "We're tak'ing a jet."

"Well, that's fun, isn't it?"

He shook his head. "Na."

"Are you going far?"

He shrugged.

"It's just Vegas," said Catriona plucking the check from Anne's fingers. "Thanks. I'll let you know the amount as soon as I know."

Anne shrugged, which Catriona found refreshing. Jeanie would have given her a checklist of hoops to jump through.

Catriona and Broch said goodbye to the temp and entered the elevator.

"Don't pack everything you own," said Catriona as the metal box lurched upward.

"Ah willnae."

"Put jeans on. No kilt."

He grunted.

"Don't bring shampoo, they'll have that there if we need to stay overnight."

"But ah lik' my shampoo."

"Do not bring it. No soap either."

"But ah ordered a new one from the jungle and it smells lik' coconuts."

Catriona shook her head. "I told you, Amazon is not a *jungle*. I mean it *is*, but not the one you order from." She frowned. The Highlander had gotten *way* too good with computers. She'd shown him how to order things he needed from Amazon and her monthly bill had quadrupled. That was fine since for the time being she cashed his checks for him, but at some point, she needed to untangle their finances before he ruined her with his hygiene-product budget. Growing up in filthy ancient Scotland had scarred the man for life.

He did smell like a morning stroll through a tropical garden. A *manly* tropical garden.

Her gaze drifted down to the veins in his arms roping toward the back of his large, beautiful hands—

She cleared her throat and looked away.

Back to business.

"Just bring a pair of jeans, a couple of shirts, and your toothbrush."

"And mah lotion."

"They'll have lotion."

"Nae *mah* lotion."

Catriona gave up as the doors slid open. "Whatever. Just hurry."

He blocked her path and peered down at her, his right eyebrow arched.

"Are ye certain we're nae married already?"

"What are you talking about?"

"The way ye *nag* me."

Catriona huffed and pushed past him, keeping her head down to hide her amusement. She stopped at her door to slip in her key. Before she could turn the knob, Broch approached, patting her butt as he passed.

She jumped and turned to squint at him.

"*Harassment*," she said.

Broch searched his sporran for his key, refusing to look at her.

"Hm? Are ye talking tae me?" he asked.

"You should put your money where your mouth is."

"Ah don't ken whit that means," he sing-songed before entering his apartment.

Catriona let herself into her home and headed for her closet. The outfit she'd chosen for the day seemed too casual to wear to Vegas, so she undressed and stood in her underwear staring at her closet.

She didn't think she needed anything fancier than jeans and a top; hopefully, they'd only be in Vegas for about an hour. She flipped through her few dresses thinking maybe it would be a good idea to bring *one* nicer thing, just in case. They needed to find Tyler, grab him, and get back, but maybe they could sneak in a nice meal there somewhere—

"Whit's that?"

Catriona whirled and covered her chest with crisscrossed arms like a vampire in her coffin.

"What the—"

Broch stood behind her shirtless and in his kilt, a pair of jeans in each hand.

She eyed his massive pecs.

That chest—I want to play it like the bongos...

"You can't walk in here unannounced," she scolded.

He shrugged. "Ye see me in mah underwear all the time."

"That's *different.*"

"Howfur?"

"I can't *avoid* you in your underwear. Hell, I'm lucky if you're *that* dressed, you exhibitionist."

"Whit's that?" he pointed at her leg.

She glanced down. "What's what?"

"The scar oan the back of yer thigh."

Catriona twisted her head to look down at her leg. A two-inch scar she'd forgotten about stared back at her. "I forget. Some accident."

"Howfur?"

"I don't remember."

"While working?"

She shrugged. "Probably."

Broch took a step forward, staring at the scar, his lips pressed into a tight line. "Yer lucky ah came."

"What do you mean?"

"Yer job is tae dangerous fer a lassie alone."

Catriona returned her attention to her closet. "I was doing just fine without you, thank you very much."

She heard the jeans drop to the floor and felt Broch step behind her to trace her scar with his finger. His feather touch on her thigh made her suck in a breath.

"I can see that," he whispered in her ear.

She swallowed. "You know what you're doing. Cut it out."

"Are ye sayin' ye dinnae need me?"

"*Yes*. That's *exactly* what I'm saying and we don't have time for these games."

His hand slid across her lower back and around her hip, his fingertips slipping under the hem of her panties.

"Are ye sure?" he whispered.

She took a ragged inhale and turned to face him, his hand sliding across her abdomen to her opposite hip.

Ohmygod that felt delicious.

She considered just twirling in place with his hands on her.

She rested a hand on his left pec. "Do you need *me*?" she asked.

He smiled. "Ye ken ah dae."

Their lips met as he cupped her rear and lifted her to him. Wrapping her legs around his waist, she threw her head back to gasp for air as he pressed his face into her breasts.

She wanted him so badly. She knew he wouldn't follow through. He was teasing her, trying to coax her into agreeing to marriage, but she couldn't seem to find the urge to stop him.

Not with her body wrapped around his.

I'm going to feel like an idiot in about five minutes, but right now...

Broch walked her toward her bed and eased her back onto it, his bulgy arms lowering her without strain.

She sat up and slid her hands up his thighs beneath his kilt.

"Marry me," he said.

Aaaand...there it is.

She thunked her forehead against his abs.

"Why did you have to say that?" She slid her hands back down to his knees.

"Just say *aye*."

She looked up at him. "I told you I can't do that. We haven't known each other long enough."

"Don't ye want me?"

"I do—"

She took a deep breath.

You have no idea.

"—but I can't marry you. Not now. Marriage is *permanent*. At least it's supposed to be."

He looked hurt. As usual. He stroked her cheek with his hand.

"Ye ken ah love ye."

"So make love *to* me."

She wasn't sure what shocked her more, that she'd shared her thoughts so blatantly, or that she'd used the phrase *make love*. So corny, but somehow, it had felt like the right thing to say.

Broch straightened and stared out the window behind her. "Mibbee."

"*Maybe?*"

"*Mibbee.* Ah'm nae sure yet."

"Could you decide in the next minute or so?"

He shook his head and stepped back, smoothing his kilt where it had begun to tent.

She took a deep breath and pointed to the door. "Then get out of here. Pack the jeans that were in your left hand and wear the ones that were in your right. Go wait by the elevator. I'll be there in a second."

He nodded and left the room, but not before he put a hand on either side of her face and gave her a loud, smacky kiss on the mouth.

Wiseass.

When he was gone, Catriona rolled over and pushed her face into her pillow to scream.

CHAPTER NINE

Catriona and Broch reached Vegas by three p.m., with Broch gripping the arms of his seat during much of the hour-long flight. He let go long enough to gulp down three shots of whiskey, spaced evenly throughout the flight.

He *hated* flying.

A car took them to Las Vegas Boulevard, —already alive with lights and color. Their destination was easy to find, a large golden obelisk serving as the dot beneath the exclamation point of the Vegas strip.

Catriona motioned to the name of the building. "It's called *Gold*, not *the golden tower*. Sean had it wrong. That's a relief."

Broch felt like he was missing something, but before he could ask for an explanation, he found his attention captured by the world outside the taxi windows. He gaped as he unfolded himself from the car, his mouth hanging open.

"Ah don't ken whaur tae look first."

"It can be a bit overwhelming." Catriona yanked her luggage from the trunk. The driver had popped it open from his seat but not bothered to help them retrieve it.

Broch knew he should help Catriona, but he couldn't pull his focus from the buildings and people around him.

Sae many lights.

As Catriona struggled to get both bags to the curb, Broch returned to earth and grabbed one with each paw to cart them into the giant golden building. He might have stared at the Strip all day but didn't want to give Catriona time to notice how heavy his luggage was.

He'd packed his lotion, the shampoo, *and* conditioner.

Inside Gold, Catriona glanced at the front desk and then led him into an elevator. Broch watched her lift a finger to push the uppermost button. Instead, she tapped the keyhole next to it and grunted.

"Shoot."

She walked back out of the elevator and he followed, the door closing enough to catch his shoulder as he hurried out. It hurt.

"Och—whaur ye gaun?"

"Elevator doesn't go to the penthouse...ah... Nope." She made it halfway through her thought before pirouetting and heading back into the closing elevator. Broch made an about-face and jumped inside, this time catching his opposite shoulder against the doors as they bounced off him and sprang open.

He rubbed his arm. "Whit noo? Yer chippin' away at me."

"If we go to the desk and ask to talk to Alain, it'll give him time to get away and maybe take Tyler with him. I've decided to do this the hard way."

"Whit's the hard way?"

"We go to the floor below the penthouse, go up the fire escape stairs and then find a way to get through the door there, which is undoubtedly locked."

Broch nodded. "By *find a way*, dae ye mean *me*?"

She smiled. "Aye."

The elevator doors opened and Broch dragged the bags down a carpeted hallway until they found the stairs leading to the penthouse behind a door labeled *fire exit*.

Catriona motioned to the luggage. "Leave the suitcases here for a sec."

Broch stared down at the bags in his hand.

"Whit if someone takes them?"

"Then we'll buy new clothes."

Broch frowned. Setting down the cases, he unzipped his and pulled his kilt from inside to tie it around his waist.

She cocked her head. "Really?"

"Cannae risk it," he mumbled as they mounted the stairs to the locked door Catriona had predicted would be there.

"Get that open," she said, motioning to the door.

He looked at the door. "Howfur am ah supposed tae dae that?"

"It's just *how*, not *howfur*. And I don't know howfur."

He squinted one eye. "How come dae ye think *ah* dae?"

"You're big. Just break it down or something. Go beast-mode."

Broch grimaced. Catriona had been cranky ever since their time in her bedroom. He suspected he knew why, but he also suspected she'd hit him if he voiced his theory.

Safer tae open the door.

He traced the edge of the door frame with his finger. "It swings this way. Ah cannae pat mah shoulder tae it." He knocked on it. "Soonds solid."

Catriona shrugged without looking up from her phone.

Broch put his finger on her phone and pushed it down. "Hey thare, lassie."

"Yes?"

"Ah ken yer takin' me fae granted."

"Really? You said I *needed* you for your mighty mighty muscles. So *use* them."

Ah.

She was trying to teach him a lesson.

Funny lass.

"Ah said ah'm nice tae hae around, ah didnae sae ah cuid solve *every* problem."

Catriona put her face so close to his he could smell her breath. It smelled like the cranberry juice she'd had on the jet.

"You said I *needed* those muscles. Without you I'm a poor defenseless little lassie."

He leaned back and crossed his arms against his chest. "Ah didnae say that."

Smirking, Catriona put her hands on his upper arms, pushing and pulling on him in an attempt to make him move. He allowed her to position him in front of the door, a few steps back, too far to reach the locked knob, his heels hovering at the top of the stairs.

"Stay there. Use his momentum."

"*Whit?*"

Broch pondered Catriona's cryptic instructions as she pounded on the door, screaming in a high-pitched voice unlike her own.

"You let me in right now Alain or I'm going to tell everyone about us. I swear Alain! I know you're in there, you—"

Broch heard a bang as someone hit the door's release bar on the opposite side. Catriona jumped back, grabbing the knob on their side and swinging the door open as she tucked herself behind it.

Broch's eyes grew wide as a man stumbled toward him, jerked off-balance by Catriona's yanking of the knob.

Use his momentum. Ah...

Broch stepped aside and pushed the man past him, flinging him down the stairs with little effort.

The man rolled to a stop at the base of the stairs and groaned, pressing one palm into the ground in an attempt to stand.

Broch looked at Catriona and she pointed to the man at the bottom of the stairs with her eyes.

"Whit? He cannae gae thro' the door wance we gae thro'."

"But he can go to the elevator. He probably has the key for the penthouse."

"Sae why don't *ye* tak' care of him?"

She shrugged. "Because I have to hold the door open so we don't get locked out again."

Och.

"Ne'ermind. Ah'll dae it."

He stomped down the stairs, grabbed a fistfull of hair on the back of the man's head, and banged his skull into the floor.

The man collapsed to his belly, still.

Broch pounded back up the stairs.

"Ye cuidhae given me a wee mair instruction afair ye threw a man at me."

Catriona smiled. "What? You did fine."

"*Fine.*"

She walked into the hall and he followed after a final glance at the unconscious man at the bottom of the stairs. He didn't appear to be going anywhere soon.

"I told you I could get the door open without you," Catriona said as they walked down the hallway.

Broch scoffed. "Bit 'twas *me* wha teuk that man tae ground."

"But *I* got the door open. Any lunkhead can *hit* someone." In the hallway, she knocked on a door across from the elevator.

Broch frowned and glanced back down the hall. He had half a mind to go wake the man and see how she liked it *then* without his help.

The door opened, revealing a small-boned woman with short, dark hair. She cocked an eyebrow at them.

"Look what the cat dragged in," she said.

Catriona offered a tight smile. "Hello, Dez."

"Hello, Catriona."

"Alain here?"

Dez leaned forward and peered down the hall.

"Looking for your man?" asked Catriona. "He's taking a nap in the stairwell."

Dez huffed, but took a step back to allow them entry.

Broch heard the boy blubbering the moment they entered the room. Tyler sat tied to a chair in the corner, farthest from the floor to ceiling windows overlooking the Strip. His eyes were puffy and red.

Upon seeing them enter, the young actor straightened and gasped.

"Cat! You have to help me. They're *crazy*. Look what they did to me."

"It's Ms. Phoenix to you after this stunt," said Catriona as she and Broch moved to Tyler.

One leg of the boy's shorts had been pushed up against his pelvis and tucked under. Blood trails ran down the sides of his thighs. The word *bum* had been carved into his leg with a very fine blade. Broch spotted the likely instrument sitting on a stone counter nearby.

Catriona glowered over her shoulder at Dez, who shrugged.

A man's voice spoke behind them.

"Cahtriona, dear. Sean said you were on your way. I left word at ze desk to let you up."

"Sae we could hae taken the elevator," muttered Broch.

Dez remained in the open doorway. She caught Alain's eye. "You okay with them? I'm going to check on Philip."

Alain waved her on and returned his attention to his visitors. "How can I help you?"

Catriona flopped her hand in Tyler's direction. "You have something of ours."

"Not at ze moment, he isn't."

Catriona reached into her pocket to retrieve a folded square of paper. "I brought a check. What does he owe you?"

Tyler sobbed, his chin dropping to his chest. "Thank you. *Ohmygod.* Thank you. I'll pay you back."

Alain waved a hand at Tyler to shut up as he eyeballed Broch. "Who's your friend, Catriona?"

"This is Brochan."

Alain nodded slowly. Broch could almost see the gears in the wee man's head grinding, and he didn't like it. He *did* like

Alain's suit, though he feared that much cream color would look strange on a frame as large as his. The Frenchman looked like a neat, wee cloud. He smelled of bergamot, which reminded Broch of a cereal he liked. His stomach growled and he regretted not eating on the plane.

Alain pointed at him, swinging his finger to point from head to toe. "My wife would love him."

"He's not for sale and he doesn't gamble."

"Lately," mumbled Broch. To be honest, he'd gambled quite a bit back in Scotland with his rich friend Gavin. It was the best way to make some quick money.

Catriona bypassed his confession and held up the check for Alain to see. "How much?" She headed into the kitchen and opened a drawer. "All I need is a pen. I think I remember how to write one of these things..."

In response to Catriona's query, Alain swatted the air, the same gesture he'd used to dismiss Dez. Broch couldn't remember a moment the man wasn't waving at someone. It was as if he were plagued by a cloud of invisible gadflies.

"Put your check away. You've given me an idea."

Catriona ceased searching through the kitchen drawers. "I don't like the sound of that. I'd rather write you a check."

"I won't take your money."

"Come on..."

Alain shook his head. "You are a resourceful girl. Do me a favor and I'll release ze boy. After, you can require he pay you for your services or not. Zat is up to you."

Staring at the floor, Catriona pinched the bridge of her nose. "Fine. What's the favor?"

"Bring my wife back to me."

Catriona looked up. "Mo? Where is she?"

Alain looked away and raised his chin to strike a dramatic pose. He fell short of holding the back of his wrist to his forehead.

"She has left me."

"Why? What did you do?"

"*Nothing.*"

"I bet. You don't know where she is?"

"I know where she ees. I need someone to convince her to come back to me."

"How am I supposed to do that?"

"You'll figure eet out eef you want ze boy back."

Catriona looked at Tyler. "I need the boy back by Monday."

Alain sniffed. "Zen I would hurry."

The door opened and Broch stepped out of the way as Dez entered, butt-first, dragging the unconscious body of her partner behind her. She pulled him into the room and dropped his arms to the ground. Puffing, she leaned against the wall to catch her breath.

Alain peered at his fallen soldier and then back at Broch. "You did ziss?"

Broch bobbed his head in Catriona's direction. "Ah'm nae sure. Ask her, she micht hae dane it all oan her own."

Catriona closed her eyes and tilted her face to the ceiling. "I swear, listening to you two destroy the English language is giving me a headache." She pointed at Alain. "Tell me where I can find Mo."

"She's at hair design studio."

"She's getting her hair done?"

With a huff, Alain pulled a pad of paper and pen from a drawer in the sofa's end table.

"*There's* the pen," grumbled Catriona.

Alain jotted down an address before thrusting the paper at Catriona. "*Hair* design studio."

"Oh. *Her* design studio. Got it. Seriously Alain, you've been here for like twenty years. Lose the accent. You're worse than Arnold Schwarzenegger. At least Broch has an excuse—he just got here."

She snatched the paper from Alain's hands and motioned to Broch.

"Let's go."

Tyler wailed, his eyes wild. "No. *Wait!* What about me?"

Catriona stopped to glare at Alain. "No more body graffiti."

Alain closed his eyes and stuck his nose in the air. "One for every day he doesn't pay."

Catriona shook her head. "Uh-uh. *No more cutting.* He has one more mark on him when I get back and I swear I'll set Mo up with the first multi-millionaire I can find."

Alain gasped, appearing genuinely concerned.

"And untie him. Get Dez to keep an eye on him. He won't run. Will you Tyler?"

Tyler sniffed. "No. I swear. My arms are killing me."

Alain sighed.

Catriona nodded and returned her attention to the

Frenchman.

"Promise me, Alain."

The little man flopped into the sofa like a petulant teenager.

"Fine."

CHAPTER TEN

Sean waved to Fernando, Parasol Picture's gatekeeper for the day, as he rolled off the lot in his beloved Jaguar. He'd bought it a few years after arriving in Los Angeles, via 1721 Scotland.

He knew all too well how confused Broch must have been when he appeared in Hollywood.

When Sean arrived, he'd been dazed both by the time travel and the knowledge that his wife and infant boy had been killed by his enemy, Thorn Campbell. If he'd known then that baby Broch had somehow survived, well, who knew. It might have been worse for him knowing he'd abandoned his son—unwillingly or not.

After nearly thirty years of reflection, he suspected he'd *allowed* his death to happen. There was no reason for him to lose his sword fight with Thorn Campbell. He'd been reckless and all but begged the man to run him through.

He hadn't wanted to live without Isobel and his boy.

But then, here he was. Alive in Hollywood. His wife and son, dead or alive, hundreds of years in the past. It hadn't felt as if they were far away at the time. He'd worn his grief like a yoke for years, but somehow he'd found the strength to start a new life in a new time. And for whatever reason, the moment he'd seen that 1969 Jaguar Series II E-Type OTS convertible, he knew his new life included it. The car was one of the few pleasures he'd allowed himself in those early years.

Landing on the Parasol Pictures lot had been lucky. Even luckier, Luther found him. Luther was Parasol's entire security force back then. He could have had Sean arrested. Instead, he'd helped him, whether or not he believed Sean's lies and later his confessions of time travel.

Good old Luther. They'd been through a lot since then.

Sean eased the brakes of the Jag, stopping at the threshold between the outer lot and the street.

Something doesn't feel right.

With a subtle movement of his head, he peered into his side-view mirror.

There it was. *Movement.* A man sat in a car behind him in the lot. A gray Lexus. His gloved fingers tapped on the wheel.

He couldn't make out the man's face, but he felt his eyes on him.

Rune.

Catriona and Fiona's father.

Has to be.

Sean hit the gas and screeched into traffic. Keeping an eye in his rearview mirror, he spotted the Lexus as it pulled from the lot and turned in his direction.

Rune's pursuit came as no surprise. Since Catriona had told him about her father visiting Fiona's hospital room, he'd known their paths would cross. After all, he'd nearly cut the man in two trying to save little Catriona from his grasp.

Chances weren't good Rune was willing to let that go.

After their battle, the gaunt, specter of a man had disappeared, presumably time-jumping to heal. But to come back? Sean had never had any control over where he appeared. Could Rune's reappearance be a coincidence?

Catriona and Broch were safe in Las Vegas. That was good.

I need to finish this before they get back.

Sean drove toward the desert until he could pull down a road where he knew traffic would be scarce. The Lexus made the same turn and followed, pacing a hundred yards behind him.

Sean pulled over, the Jag's tires crunching on the soft dirt.

The Lexus arrived a few moments later. It slowed, and then drifted to the roadside, parking twenty feet behind him.

No more pretending.

They sat in their cars for five minutes. Sean counted the seconds. He couldn't stop looking at his watch.

Patient bastard.

Tired of waiting, Sean opened his door and stepped out. He turned to face his pursuer.

The Lexus door opened and a lanky man stepped out. Wearing a plaid shirt buttoned high on his neck, and jeans that made his skinny limbs look like spider legs, he stood staring at Sean.

"You look like a cartoon cowboy," said Sean to break the ice. The man didn't answer.

"I know you're Fiona's father. Rune. That's your name?" Rune nodded.

"What do you want?" Sean shifted his weight from one leg to the other. He didn't like doing all the talking. Catriona would have laughed to see him as the chatty one.

Rune's gloved hand lifted and slipped behind him. When it reappeared, it held a gun.

Shite.

Sean hadn't considered gunplay an option. His gun sat in his desk drawer back at the office.

Stupid.

Rune fired. Sean ducked and scrambled to hide below the front of his car.

Firing a second time, Rune paced forward.

Sean looked behind him. Nowhere to run except down the road. He'd be an easy target.

I can't just sit here, waiting for him to show up.

Sean shifted to the side of the car and slipped into the passenger seat.

Rune continued to advance.

A bullet crashed through the back window of the Jaguar and whizzed inches from Sean's head before embedding in the dash.

Not the Jag. Sonovabitch.

Sean threw his legs into the driver's side and hit the gas as he slammed the car into gear. The driver's side window shattered, the bullet grazing his arm. He heard the sand beneath the outer wheel grind until the driver side tire caught, shooting the car forward. Sean wrestled the vehicle to the road.

Something thudded against the side of the car. Sean glanced in the rearview to find Rune spinning toward the middle of the road, trying to find his feet. While pulling from the roadside, Sean had clipped his hip.

He'd been that close to a bullet in the head.

Sean's attention moved from the spinning man to the enormous thing barreling down behind him. The eighteen-wheeler roared toward Rune.

Rune had no idea.

The truck's brakes screamed as Rune stumbled into its path.

Too late.

Through his broken windows, Sean heard the thud. Rune flew skyward, tossed like a rag doll.

Sean slammed on his brakes. He thrust his head through the shattered driver's side window to watch Rune's body as it arced through the air.

He never landed.

Sean blinked, wondering how he'd lost sight of the man.

There was no second thud as the body hit the pavement.

The truck came to a stop, nearly jackknifing in the middle of the road. The driver jumped down from his cab and ran to the front of his rig. He spun, arms outstretched on either side of him, mouth gaping, searching for the man he'd struck.

Time to leave.

While Sean *had* considered throwing the Jag into reverse and running over Rune to ensure the bastard's need to travel far, far away—the ghoul never landed. Disappearing mid-air didn't work within the laws of physics and therefore, *couldn't be good.* He might have escaped to another time—slunk off, so someday he could pop up again like a reoccurring case of heartburn.

Sean shifted into gear and hit the gas. He felt confident he was already far enough away the trucker wouldn't be able to read his plate. That poor man would be lucky if he remembered anything about Sean's vehicle, considering he'd struck a man with a vehicle the size of a small train.

Sean gripped the wheel at ten and two.

Could it have been that easy?

Foe arrives, and the foe is hit by a truck. Hopefully, Catriona wouldn't be upset about her father's second death, though it didn't seem as though she wanted anything to do with—

A man appeared in the road in front of Sean.

The figure held a gun pointed at him.

Rune.

How—?

A bullet-sized hole appeared in his windshield. Sean didn't swerve. Rune didn't move.

Sean pressed the gas to the floor.

Let's see how you like being run over twice, you son of a—

A second gunshot echoed seconds before he struck the

man.

The last thing Sean remembered was a crack in his windshield, right in front of his field of vision.

Oh no.

Not the Jag.

CHAPTER ELEVEN

Catriona and Broch gathered their luggage and returned to the front desk to check their bags. Catriona doubted they'd solve all Alain's problems with Mo before nightfall, but hope sprang eternally.

The Gold wouldn't let them store their bags with no promise of securing a room, so Catriona produced her studio credit card. She hoped Mo would cooperate. They'd be finished their mission in an hour, and then she, Broch, and Tyler could head home. She didn't want to find herself in a hotel room with Kilty for the evening, making a fool out of herself while he strode around his moral high ground.

No. She was done trying to pull him off his high horse. Either he'd come to her or she was *done.*

Just think about work. Work, work, work.

"We're going to need to get another taxi to—"

Catriona didn't feel Broch's presence behind her and the man behind the counter stared at her as if she'd been talking to him.

She turned to find the Highlander gone.

Catriona pushed the two suitcases behind the desk, took her receipt, and scanned the lobby for her missing partner. She spotted Broch near the front door talking to a man making strangely stylized hand gestures.

Magician. Broch had been accosted by a lobby magician.

The roaming entertainer turned his head to pop a blue ball from his mouth. She spotted his white face and grimaced.

Worse.

A *mime* magician.

Catriona strode to Broch, thrusting his luggage ticket at

him. "Put this in your pocket. It claims our luggage behind the desk there. We have to go."

"Cat, he made a ball disappear fae his hand and appear in his gob."

She nodded. "Yep. He's a magician. That's what they do. Gargle balls all day."

The mime scowled at her and held up an index finger. Not the finger she'd expected after her comment. He was asking them to wait. He pointed to Broch's jeans pocket.

"Whit? Mah pocket?" Broch slid his fingers inside and pulled out a shiny wad of paper. He unfolded it and gasped.

"Tis a *eight* of spades. That wis mah card. Ah picked it afore ye—"

Catriona rolled her eyes. "Right. Amazing. Let's go."

"But he cam tae shaw me his magic," protested Broch as she dragged him away.

"That's because he has no friends. That's why he became a magician in the first place."

The mime held up his middle finger for her to see.

There it is.

"Nice. *Classy* mime." Catriona dragged Broch toward the door.

"Thank ye," Broch called over his shoulder, holding aloft the folded card. "Thank ye, wizard."

The mime nodded and waved, shooting Catriona a final glare in response to her interrupting his chance at earning a tip.

They walked outside and the desert heat quickly warmed their air-conditioned skin.

"Whyfur were ye sae mean tae the painted wizard?"

Catriona sighed. "I'm sorry. I wasn't trying to be mean. We have work to do and mimes freak me out. Anything clown-like. I don't like people in costumes, but especially clowns."

"Ah thoght he was a clever jester." He poked her in the arm. "Ye need tae hae more *fun*."

She scoffed. "I keep trying to have fun and you keep shooting me down."

He stared at her a moment and then smirked. "Ah. Ah see whit yer sayin'. Mibbie we cuid git merit 'ere, eh? Ah saw a sign—"

"Right. As soon as we get Tyler."

Broch perked. "Aye?"

"No."

He frowned.

The hotel's doorman flagged them a car to take them to Mo's design studio. Broch pressed his face against the glass, staring up at the billboards and flashing marquees.

"Excalibur," he read aloud. "They hae sword fighting. Kin we gae there?"

"Sure. When Tyler is safe."

"Aye?"

"No."

Broch fell silent again. "Whit's a Spearmint Rhino?"

Catriona snorted a laugh. "It's a strip club. Men go there to watch women dance naked."

He blinked at her. "Vegas is *mad*."

"That's why they call it Sin City."

Broch grunted and blinked at the sign as they passed. "The lassie is bonnie though."

"It's a high-end place. The dancers are all tens."

"Tens?"

"It's a stupid old rating scale for looks. One to ten, ten being the best-looking."

"Ah." He looked at her. "Ah think yer a ten."

Catriona felt her cheeks warm and she felt a wave of embarrassment to be flattered by such a silly compliment.

She looked away and let it go.

They left the lights and glitter of the Strip and traveled several miles into the desert to an industrial park. The taxi rolled in front of a large warehouse with the word *Modacious* mounted to the front wall. The M and O were in red, the rest of the letters in black script.

Broch and Catriona moved from air conditioning to heat to air conditioning again in the warehouse. Inside, rows of clothing on racks created life-sized mazes with people milling in and out, swatches of fabric, dresses, and half-finished tops in their hands. In one corner, a tailor pinned a dress worn by a statuesque redhead and Broch stopped to admire her. She waved and he waved back.

"Does *she* dance at the Rhino?" he asked Catriona.

She chuckled. "I doubt it and don't ask her."

In the back corner sat an office area, fashioned to look like a quaint cottage built inside the larger warehouse. The walls were glass, allowing those inside to monitor warehouse activity.

Catriona headed toward the office, knocking on the glass

door to catch the attention of a tall, curvy older woman with bleach-blonde hair coiled atop her head. The woman turned, forehead scrunching behind her large round glasses as she peered over the frames. She motioned for a mousy young woman beside her to open the door.

"Can I help you?" asked the girl.

"I need to speak to Mo."

"She's not in. Can I take a message?"

Catriona glanced at Mo, who stood staring back at her, her already overly plumped lips, pursed.

Catriona turned back to the girl.

"I'm looking right at her."

The girl shook her head. "She's unavailable."

Catriona rolled her eyes and pushed her head inside. She was taller than Mo's assistant and there was little the girl could do to stop her without throwing her hands above her head and blocking her like a goal-tending basketball player.

"Mo, it's Catriona. Sean Shaft's daughter. I work for Parasol Pictures...we met a long time ago."

Mo's expression expanded into a smile as she moved to the door, pushing the mousy girl aside.

"Catriona, I deedn't recahgnize you. You were a teenahgair ze lahst time I sahw you."

Mo threw her arms around Catriona. Catriona took the opportunity to whisper into the fashion designer's ear.

"Please drop the accent. I can't take it anymore. You'll see why in a second."

Mo released her and pointed to her worker. "You. Out."

The minion scurried away and Catriona and Broch entered the office. The temperature felt ten degrees colder inside.

Mo patted Catriona on the arm. "How did you know my little secret?" she said, her French lilt replaced by something decidedly more Midwest. "It's a pain, but people buy my clothes faster when they think I'm French and not from some Podunk town in Northwest Michigan."

"I remember you and Sean talking when I was little." In truth, Catriona mostly remembered Sean laughing while watching an interview with Mo using her cartoonish French accent on television.

Mo fanned herself. "Oh, your *father*. What a sexy, sexy man he was. *Is,* probably. Is he married now? I might have an opening..."

"No. And that's what I came to talk to you about."

Mo turned her attention to Broch. "And who's this? He looks a lot like—"

"A young Sean. I know. Broch is Sean's son, and the primary accent in my life at the moment."

"Enchante," said Mo, holding out a hand.

Broch took it and kissed the back of it.

"Tis lovely tae mak yer acquaintance."

Mo pretended to shiver with delight. "Oh, he sounds like Sean Connery, only even manlier, if that's possible."

Catriona rolled her eyes.

"He makes me wish I designed men's clothing. I could dress and undress him all day. I missed out on the old stag, maybe I should set my sights on the young buck?" Mo giggled and slapped Catriona lightly on the shoulder. "So what's up, sweetheart? I assume you didn't come here just to bring me *him*?"

"No. I need a favor."

"Anything. What can I do for you?"

"I need you to go back to Alain."

Mo's expression darkened, her smile disappearing as if her facial muscles had been shot with Botox. "Go back to that hunk of moldy camembert? Forget it. He's embarrassed me for the last time."

"What did he do?"

"I spotted him with a woman wearing one of *my* dresses before it was available for sale. *He* gave it to her. I know he did. *She was just his type.*"

Catriona shook her head. "Oh come on. Alain worships you. He'd never do that." Catriona had no idea if that was true, but it sounded good.

Mo lifted her nose into the air. "That's what *he* said. But who else could have given her the dress?" She wrapped her arms around her chest and stared off into the warehouse as if she were standing in a stiff breeze atop the bluffs, awaiting her sailor's return. Catriona could almost hear the music swelling. After a moment of posing, her attention snapped back to them. "Did I tell you she was his type?"

Catriona nodded. "You did. What if I could prove Alain didn't do it?"

Mo lifted her hands into the air. "Why? What do you care about my relationship with Alain?"

"He's got one of our actors on a poker debt. He wants you back in exchange for our boy."

"Like I'm *property*?"

Whoops. Catriona winced. *Probably shouldn't have told her that.*

"Not like property, like you're more important than money. He wouldn't take my check. He said only you could make him happy again."

Mo scoffed. "Make him happier than money? Now I know you're lying." Mo looked away, but Catriona could see the idea of Alain preferring her over cash had softened her resolve.

"I'm not lying. I swear. He only wants you back."

"Oh. Well..." Somehow, Mo raised her chin another notch to peer down her nose at Catriona. "So he wants a favor in exchange for what you want?"

Oh no. Catriona sensed Mo's gears churning. She tried to steamroller forward.

"Right, so if you could go back to him, even if it's just long enough for me to get Tyler—"

"*I* want a favor."

Other. Shoe. Dropped.

Catriona felt her shoulders slump. She spoke her words as if she'd carried them, strapped to her back, all the way to the conversation.

"What do you need?"

Mo strolled to the glass window and tapped a pen against it. "Someone's selling my clothes."

"That's a good thing, isn't it?"

"*Last year's* clothes. The ones that should be burned."

"Burned? Don't be so hard on yourself—"

Mo scowled. "Not burned because they're *bad*, burned because I need to create *demand*. The stores send me back what they haven't sold and I burn them rather than let them be sold discount. It creates a sense of scarcity and drives up my prices."

Catriona gasped. "Oh my god, that's terrible. What a *waste*."

Mo shrugged. "It's a necessary evil. All the big labels do it."

"So you're saying someone is stealing the clothes earmarked for burning and selling them?"

"Yes. I need it stopped."

Catriona realized she hadn't seen Broch in a bit and glanced behind her. He'd wandered to a table in the back of the office to wrap a plaid scarf around his neck. His left arm stuck through the armhole of a ladies' sequined vest. He contorted, trying to poke the other arm through the opposite side without ripping the fabric.

He noticed her watching him and smiled.

"Ah think ah need a larger size. Ah lik' the sparkles."

Catriona sighed and turned her attention back to Mo. "It can't be hard to figure out who's stealing the clothes, can it? I mean, who's doing the collecting and the burning?"

Without batting an eye, Mo pulled a larger vest off the rack behind her and tossed it to Broch. "That's just it. I thought I could solve the problem by changing shipping companies, but it happened again this year. They're robbing the trucks—paying off the workers—I don't know. That's what I need you to figure out. My clothes show up in these underground pop-up stores but they've always packed up and left before I hear about them."

Catriona looked at her watch. She was running out of time to return Tyler for his first day of shooting. "What if I promised to solve your problem, but you go back to Alain *now*?"

"I need *this* problem solved *now*. They're flooding the market as we speak."

"But I need Tyler back on the set by Monday. That only gives me one weekend to solve this for you."

"Then you'd better hurry."

"That's what your husband said to me."

Mo sniffed. "I said he was a cheat. I never said he was stupid."

Catriona took a deep breath and exhaled. "Where should I start? Who collects the clothes and where are they sent to be burned?"

Mo motioned to her assistant, who'd been hovering outside the office space since her banishment. "Honey can get you that information. Honey!" Mo bellowed at the glass and the girl came scurrying into the room.

"Yes?"

"Get zees people ze eenfahrmahtion on who cahllects lahst year's clahthes ahnd where zey ahre sent to be burned."

"Right." She turned to Catriona. "I'll text it to you. Give me your phone."

Catriona fished her phone from her pocket and handed it to Honey, who sent herself a text. "Expect it within the next twenty minutes."

Catriona nodded and motioned to Broch that it was time to

leave. He put down a swatch of cloth he'd been rubbing against his cheek and nodded to Mo, pointing at his vest and scarf ensemble.

"Can I keep these?"

"Sure. Is your mother a curvy lady?"

Broch stared at her.

"Em... Aye?"

Mo nodded and dismissed them with a wave.

Broch motioned to the cloth he'd left behind. "That was soft. Ah lik' it. It wid make a nice neckerchief."

Mo's eyebrows raised and she glanced at the fabric.

"That's not a bad idea."

CHAPTER TWELVE

Leaving the warehouse, Catriona stopped so suddenly Broch bumped into the back of her.

"Och, ye cannae stoap in the middle o' the door."

"Sorry. Our car is gone." Catriona pulled down the sunglasses she'd dropped from their perch atop her head and scanned the parking lot for signs of their taxi. "That's not good."

"We kin call another, eh?"

"Yes, but that was a real taxi, not like the cars you call back in Los Angeles. He hadn't been paid yet. Why would he leave?"

"Maybe his wife is having a baby and the child is a breach."

Catriona squinted at him. "That seems wildly specific."

Broch shrugged. "Maybe his boy accidentally cut himself on an ax while chopping firewood."

Catriona shook her head as she pulled her phone from her pocket. "Life in old-timey Scotland sure sounds fun. I'm glad I don't remember it. Next, you're going to tell me his mother came down with the plague."

"It's possible."

"No, it's *not*, that's my point—"

Catriona's phone rang in her hand before she could call for a new car. Answering, she heard Alain's accent on the opposite end.

"Hello, beautiful."

She scowled. "Don't *hello beauteeful* me, Alain. Thanks to you, I have to solve all of your wife's problems now too. I need you to let Tyler—"

"I'm going to let him go."

Catriona paused. "You are?"

"Oui. I did. Dez ees taking him to ze airport as we speak."

"I brought the studio's jet here to pick him up."

"Oh. Well, too late. He has a ticket now. He ees going home."

Catriona nodded, feeling the weight on her shoulders grow a little lighter. "Okay. That works. Thanks, Alain. How much do I owe you again? I'll bring the check right now."

Alain's tone shifted to dismissive. She could almost hear him waving her away from his side of the phone. "Don't worry about eet. I'm going to consider ziss a learning experience for ze boy. He can pay me back over time. I'm not in any hurry." Alain sniffed. "I'm rich."

The feeling that began as *relief*, sprouted hairy legs and crawled up Catriona's neck as *suspicion*.

Something isn't right.

The taxi left without being paid. Then, Alain—who'd been so determined to teach Tyler a lesson he'd carved a word on the boy's thigh—happily let him go *and* bought him a plane ticket home.

It was as if while they were inside talking to Mo, the whole world had been rotated one hundred and eighty degrees on a lazy-Susan.

Deep in thought, Catriona dragged the scarf off Broch's neck and twisted her wrist, working the long thin fabric like a limp lasso.

"Do you mind if I ask what changed your mind?" she asked Alain.

"I realized he's terrible at poker. I should keep him around, no?"

"Mm-hm. Good logic. Though I wish you'd come to that conclusion before you carved him up."

"Ah pardon, pardon. My bad."

Broch tried to reclaim his scarf and Catriona tugged it away, pacing.

"Right. Well, it's been nice doing business with you." Catriona was about to hang up when she heard Alain's voice again. She put the phone back to her ear.

"—and you don't have to run ze errand my wife has asked of you."

"Mo says so? You guys are reconciled already?"

"Oui."

Something about his *oui* didn't sound convincing. "Alain, I'm standing right outside Mo's studio door. All I need to do is poke my head back inside and confirm with her."

"Ah, no, you just don't have to. I will win her back on my own. I will root out the thief."

"I appreciate that, but how did you know it was about a thief?"

"Er... She's been complaining a long time about zat."

"Hm. Well, I gave her my word I'd figure it out for her."

"But I've let ze boy go."

"I understand that, but this is between me and Mo now. I mean, I guess I could ask her if it's okay if I let you handle it—"

"No." Alain barked his answer into the phone. "Don't bother. I will handle eet. Go home. Tell Sean I said hello."

"But—"

"*Go home.*"

"Okay—"

Alain hung up and Catriona lowered the phone from her ear. She looked at Broch, who had ducked back to press himself against the building, hiding from the sun beneath the insufficient awning that spanned the length of the industrial park. The glittery vest draped over his arm sparkled.

The heat had inspired him to remove the vest, and for that Catriona was grateful.

"That was weird." She wandered to him to take the vest and hand him the scarf. He used it to wipe the sweat from his brow.

"Whit?"

"Alain sent Tyler home."

"Oan our plane?"

"On a commercial flight."

"Oh."

Broch seemed disappointed.

"You thought if the plane left without us, we'd have to drive home."

"Aye."

"Sorry."

She stood staring at Mo's door, running through her conversation with Alain in her head. Opening the door, she caught the eye of a worker and threw the vest to them.

"Och—That wis mine."

"It was a woman's vest."

Broch pushed past her and plucked the vest from the startled worker's hands before returning outside.

He glowered at Catriona. "Ah ken it's a wummin's vest. Ah wis goan tae give it tae *Jeanie* when she comes back."

Catriona smiled. "Oh. That's so sweet."

"Ah ken. Ah'm as sweet as shortbread."

She chuckled as he folded the vest and scarf against his chest. When he was done, he eyed her.

"How come dinnae ye keek happy? Tyler goan home is guid, richt?"

She nodded. "Yes. But Alain told me not to help Mo either."

"That's double guid."

"It should be, but something about the way he said it. Something's up. I don't know if he's hiding something from Mo or—"

Catriona spotted movement and turned her head toward the parking lot. A man in a white tee-shirt and a long duster jacket leaned against a car there, smoking. She couldn't see past his sunglasses to tell if he was looking at them, but he seemed out of place in the otherwise empty parking lot. She didn't remember him there a moment before.

She turned to Broch. "Don't be obvious about it, but see the man behind me? Is it me, or is he watching us?"

Broch's gaze shifted from her face to over her shoulder.

"Ye mean the laddie walking toward us?"

"Is he? White tee, weird long jacket?"

Broch nodded. "Aye."

Catriona turned as casually as she could, pretending to be looking at her phone. Broch was right, the man had finished his cigarette and was walking toward them.

The man reached inside his coat.

"He's reaching for something." Catriona grabbed Broch's arm and pushed him ahead of her down the walkway. She continued to prod him until they were power walking along the edge of the strip mall.

The man kept coming. She spotted a piece of paper in his hand.

Not a gun.

He looked away and entered a building next to Mo's.

Exhaling, Catriona put her hand on her chest. She took two steps into the parking lot to get a better view of the building into which the man had disappeared with his loaded paper. As soon as she saw the name on it, she knew what the man had held in his hand.

A dry-cleaning ticket.

"False alarm. I guess he got his collection of duster jackets cleaned last week. Weirdo."

Broch clucked his tongue. "Yer a wee jumpy."

She nodded. "Sorry. It's Alain's tone, the taxi being gone..."

"Somethin' doesnae feel right."

"Right. It's more of a feeling than—"

A black Mercedes pulled into the parking lot, screeching on two wheels as it pulled off the main road. It rocketed toward Mo's studio and parked diagonally across two spots. All four doors opened at once and men with guns in their hands stepped out.

Catriona put a hand on Broch's chest.

"There it is."

Broch took two strides forward and pushed open the first door on his left.

"In here."

They ducked inside a Chinese restaurant. Though empty, they could hear cooking noises clanking from the back.

Catriona raised her phone. "I have to warn Mo."

Broch stared out the window. "Na ye don't."

"What?"

"They're all comin' *this* way."

"Crap."

Catriona wove through the tables and chairs toward the back of the restaurant and entered the kitchen through a hundred dangling, beaded strings. Two men looked up at her. One had been chopping vegetables, the other stood over a steaming cooktop. Neither were Asian.

"Get out, go, run." Catriona said to them, shooing at them with the back of her hand.

They stared back at her.

"¿Quién eres?" asked the one with the chopping knife.

She made a gun with her fingers. "Men are coming. Uh, hombres con pistolas."

She shot them with her finger gun and then hung her tongue out of her mouth, pretending to be dead. Jogging behind the metal countertop, she ushered them toward the back door.

"¡Ándale! Rapido!"

They looked at each other, shrugged, and sauntered out the back door.

"Mebbe we should gae out the door tae."

"Good idea."

Catriona followed the cooks to find the door opened to a thin alley. She watched as one of the workers skinnied past a man with a drawn gun. Having seen the weapon, the cooks' gait had increased accordingly and they soon disappeared around the corner of the building.

The man with the gun had no interest in the kitchen staff. He continued forward, eyes locked on Catriona.

She stepped back into the building, pushing Broch with her.

"Change of plans," she said, closing and locking the door. "Stay away from the door. They're coming."

With a rustling of plastic beads, another man appeared at the doorway leading into the kitchen from the dining room.

He raised a gun.

Before Catriona could duck, something flashed by her head and a knife handle seemed to magically appear, sticking from the gunman's shoulder. The man yelped and dropped his weapon to the floor as he spun back behind the curtain of beads and out of view.

Catriona turned in time to see Broch pulling another kitchen knife from a block.

She stared at him, wide-eyed. "You threw a *knife*?"

"Aye, but thare ur ainlie three mair. We can't keep this up a' day," he muttered. "Where's yer pistol?"

"Back at the damn hotel in my bag. I didn't think I'd need to *shoot* Alain—"

"Catriona..." a voice called from beyond the beads.

"Why does that guy know who I am?"

Broch shrugged. "He doesnae want me. Ah kin donder richt oot o' 'ere."

"Very funny." Catriona ducked down, eyes peering over the stainless steel countertop as she called back.

"What do you want?"

"Can I look around this corner without catching a knife in my forehead?"

"Maybe. No guns."

"No guns. See?"

A man's empty hands poked through the curtain, followed by a face. The man was tall, with a shaved head and sharp jawline. Catriona didn't find him familiar.

As the man moved a little farther into view she thought his

features leaned Slavic. He had an oval face and a nose a little too long for his face.

Overall, he didn't look like a whimsical guy.

"What do you want?" asked Catriona. "Who are you?"

"My name is Volkov. I'm here to ask you to go home. That is all."

"Couldn't you have done that without the guns in the first place?"

"You were already asked once and here you are."

Catriona scowled.

Alain.

Alain had asked her to go home and this man knew it.

She huffed. "Nobody gave me a chance to go home, did they? I was barely off the phone with Alain before you and your thugs showed up waving guns around like maniacs. You work for Alain?"

The man laughed. "He might think so, but it is the other way round."

Catriona frowned.

That confirms it. Alan and this guy are in cahoots.

Alain wasn't the sort of guy who worked for other people. Catriona suspected he'd gotten himself in over his head with someone. The Russian mob, perhaps, based on the look and sound of the face poking through the red beads.

"He sent you?"

"No. Our mutual interests sent me."

Another voice spoke from behind the wall and Volkov's face disappeared behind the curtain. His hands, still thrust through the beads, held up a finger.

"One moment please."

Catriona heard him talking to someone.

Volkov's face appeared once more. "I guess today is your lucky day."

Catriona nodded. "I was just thinking I should buy a lottery ticket."

He flashed her a toothy grin. "I like you. You have fire. We are going now. Do not follow us."

With that, the man disappeared behind the curtain.

Catriona remained still until she heard the bell on the restaurant's front door jingle.

She looked at Broch. "That was it? Just like that?"

Broch frowned. "How come did he leave?"

"I don't know. Everyone keeps letting us off the hook today and I don't like it. Things aren't supposed to be this easy."

"It means it's going tae get worse."

"Exactly."

Brock kept his knife and the two of them crept to the doorway. Broch held up a finger, asking her to wait, and dropped to his hands and knees. Dipping low, as if doing a pushup, he stuck his head through the beads and into the hallway before retracting it to stand.

"It's clear."

Catriona stared at him. "What the hell was that? An impromptu push-up?"

"Ah lik' tae keek aroond corners that wey. Na one ever has thair gun trained tae shoot someone's foot. By the time thay keek me and adjust, ah'm gaen."

Catriona squinted at him. "And if they run after you, you're on your hands and knees scrambling away like a raccoon?"

"Ah'm a very fast crawler."

Catriona rolled her eyes.

"Okay, forest critter, let's get out of here and get to the warehouse. I'm suddenly *very* inspired to find out what Alain is up to."

CHAPTER THIRTEEN

Sean opened his eyes to find himself staring at a gray-blue sky. Something felt very wrong. He couldn't discern *what* until a nippy breeze ruffled his hair. Goose pimples popped up their heads and waddled down his arms.

They'd been *desert* geese for decades and the chill sent them scurrying.

Sean spotted a dull glow behind the thick clouds above him.

Definitely daytime.

Southern California never felt *chilly* in the daytime.

Cold damp spread across his back, tickling his neck and making him shiver. He rolled to his left and heard the ground squish beneath him.

Cold and wet. Very unlike Southern California.

He heard the sound of people talking not far from where he lay. Something about their language didn't seem right, but he attributed it to the voices being too faint for him to make out the actual words.

Okay. One thing at a time.

He strained to sit up and then stopped, out of breath.

Och. My chest hurts.

He chuckled that he'd said *och*. Broch was rubbing off on him, bringing back the Scottish accent he'd spent so long correcting.

Sean lifted his right hand. It felt as if he were underwater, or as if Lilliputians had tied him to the ground, and every movement he made dragged the little people with him, clinging to the ropes.

I am not firing on all cylinders here.

Crawling his fingers across his ribcage like a spider, he felt for the spot that pained him the most. His fingertips located something hard just below his left pec. He traced its edges with his finger.

What could be so hard in the center of my chest?

A little voice in the back of his head answered him.

A bullet.

No. That's crazy.

Why would I think there's a bullet in my chest?

And yet... There *was* a bullet in his chest. He couldn't see it, but he felt certain.

That bastard shot me.

Even as he said the words, he wasn't sure whom he meant.

Who shot me?

He closed his eyes and tried to remember the last thing he could.

He'd been driving.

On the road, a tall, thin man stood, his arm raised.

He had a gun.

Rune.

The image of Rune grew larger and clearer by the second.

I'm going to run him down.

The gun fired. Sean saw the hole appear in his window, closer to the passenger side than his side.

He groaned.

Not the *Jag.*

First the back window, now the front—

He heard air whistling through.

The gun fired a second time. Another hole. His first thought had been *thank god he's destroying the window over and over and hasn't hit the engine block or the body.*

But then, he did hit *a* body, didn't he?

It felt as though someone had pointed a blowtorch against his breastbone and flicked on the searing flame.

He remembered now.

Rune shot him.

I must have hit him with my car?

Sean pushed himself into a sitting position. The wind iced him as it molested more of his body. He wanted to lie back down and hide from it, but he needed to move before he froze in place.

He curled his left fingers and felt the dirt give beneath them. Wet. Thick. Spongy.

I must have been thrown from the car. Maybe in a soggy ravine?

Fifty yards ahead of him people milled around low stone buildings with thatched roofs and a cluster of ramshackle booths. The scene reminded him of a California farmers' market, but no one wore yoga pants. The colors were all wrong. Everything was some variation of black, brown, and green. Muted earth tones. Much like the land around him—green and black, wet and clumpy. The air smelled fresh, though he wished it would stop assaulting his flesh with its frigid claws.

He took a deep breath.

I know that smell.

The smell told him one thing for sure.

This isn't California.

Sean heard a whistling noise.

What is that?

The noise stopped and he resumed sniffing the wind.

There it is again.

He cocked his head.

A wheezy, bubbly—

Oh.

He tucked his chin and peered down. The hard object he'd felt earlier sat there, like a tiny sheriff's badge glinting through a hole in his shirt.

The bullet hit my lung.

He fingered the bullet again and realized it protruded from his chest far enough he could grab the edges of it with his fingers. It had been deeper at one point. Of that, he felt sure. But somehow it had popped back up again like a buoy.

This is going to hurt.

He dug his nails around it and braced himself.

One, two—

He pulled it out with a sucking pop. Searing pain radiated across his chest and he gasped, falling sideways, his elbow pushing deep into the mud.

He closed his eyes as the pain slowly subsided. He'd have to be careful because he knew there would be no antibiotics for this wound. The pain had helped him realize the truth.

I jumped.

He'd been blocking the possibility from his mind, but only time travel explained the weather, the damp, and the way a bullet had punctured his lung only to pop back out far enough that he could pluck it like a found lucky penny.

His body had healed enough to live—the bullet had been pushed out of his lung—but he didn't feel reborn. He felt ragged and sore.

He took slow breaths, each deeper than the last until the wheezing subsided. It became easier to breathe. The lung sealed, but the area still ached.

Sean rolled off his elbow and stared at the people. A little village sat maybe five hundred yards from where he'd landed. From where he'd *appeared*? He wasn't sure what it looked like when he arrived, but apparently, no one had seen it.

The peasants didn't notice him even now, but he watched them and chewed on the awful truth. Unless he'd awoken on the outskirts of a renaissance festival, he could safely assume he'd gone back in time *hundreds* of years.

No medicine. No Jaguars.

No Catriona. No Broch. No Luther.

He'd only *just* been reunited with his son and now he was gone from the boy's life again. Catriona still needed time and training—

He set his jaw.

No time to dwell.

He needed to find somewhere safe to heal. He wouldn't last an evening half-soaked, lying on the cold peat.

Peat. It *was* peat surrounding him.

Could I be back in Scotland?

Groaning, he climbed to his feet. He stared a moment at his sneakers, worried what his new neighbors might think of his strange footwear. He shrugged. It didn't matter. He could make up a country from which he hailed and they'd believe him and think everyone there wore similar shoes. Their education of the world stretched only as far as their eye could see.

He could tell them he'd come from a country called New Balance.

But he couldn't be *too* strange.

Next thing I know, they'll be claiming I'm a witch.

That never ended well for the witch.

Hand on his chest, he stumbled down a shallow hill and entered the small crowd of people. A few villagers cast curious looks in his direction before hurrying on their way. He hadn't bumped into anyone in charge yet—anyone who felt they had the right to demand who he was.

He tapped the arm of a man pulling chunks of bread off a loaf to stuff them into his mouth.

"What day is this?" he asked.

Please speak English. Some of the conversations he heard around him sounded English, but others didn't. His head still felt jumbled. He wasn't sure if they were speaking in another tongue, or if his muddled head hadn't yet found a way to process what he heard.

The man snapped from his trance and looked at him. He eyeballed Sean's modern shirt, his attention falling and lingering on the sneakers before returning to his face.

"Whit day? Tis tenth October."

Sean shook his head. "I mean what *year*?"

"Whit year?" The man laughed. "Tis year o' our laird seventeen twenty-yin."

Judging from the peasant's accent, filthy tartan, and leggings...

"Scotland?" he asked, wincing at how silly he sounded.

The man peered back at him. Sean could tell his new friend's amused ridicule was morphing into uneasy suspicion. Only a man with something wrong in his head wouldn't know the year, month, day, or country. This man had no interest in talking to a lunatic.

"Aye, Glen Orchy," the man mumbled as he wandered away, clearly unconcerned his sudden departure might be read as rude.

Sean nodded.

October tenth, seventeen twenty-one, Glen Orchy.

Sean felt his skin crawl.

It couldn't be.

The day his wife had been killed by Thorn Campbell.

Sean glanced at his wrist and realized he hadn't worn a watch. He'd gotten tired of constantly checking it—it was like having a second boss, wrapped around his arm, nagging him.

Shoot. The one day I could use one...

He stopped a passing woman. "What time is it?"

The woman gave him the same odd look like the last man but raised her hand to peer at the sun. "Tis early morn."

"I still have time," he said aloud. The woman left him without asking what he meant.

Sean scanned the surrounding moors, trying to find a way to orient himself.

It couldn't be an accident.

Why would I come back to this time, this place, if it wasn't to save my wife?

He'd been given a second chance. His young self was out there, somewhere, on his way to battle Thorn. But he could go to his home—the place he should have stayed—and stop Thorn's men from murdering his wife.

Surely, he must have been to this village a million times. He'd simply forgotten. He'd been in Los Angeles for nearly thirty years.

North.

Yes. He remembered now. This village lay five miles south of his cottage.

Too far.

He couldn't walk there in time. He didn't know the exact moment his cottage had been set ablaze, but he knew it was early in the day.

Sean spotted several horses tied to stakes on the outskirts of the ramshackle market.

I can ride there in time.

Sean approached the beasts and stood petting a black one on the neck as he scanned the crowd. No one looked in his direction.

Could his old bones hop on an unsaddled horse the way they used to? Could he even stay on top of the creature?

He pulled the horse's reins from the stake and gathered them in his hand, along with a clump of mane near the horse's withers.

Here goes nothing.

With a sharp intake of breath that he regretted immediately, Sean jumped and used the horse's mane to hoist his body across its back. His chest throbbed, his breath coming in short, painful gasps. He threw a leg over the horse and sat up.

So far, so good.

Taking a moment to recall the feeling of a horse beneath his weight, he spurred on the beast. The animal broke into a trot, bouncing Sean and sending shooting pains through his chest and groin. Doubling over, he struck his mount a second time with his heels and it began to canter. That gait was easier on his body.

Okay. Settle in. You can do this. It's like riding a bike, only infinitely more painful.

Amy Vansant

He pointed the horse to the north and held on for dear life.
I'm coming, Isobel.

CHAPTER FOURTEEN

Catriona gave the address Mo's mouse had sent them to a new taxi driver and the man turned to look at them through the sliding window.

"This address is way out of town."

Catriona shrugged. "It's where we have to go."

The driver sighed and started the fare.

Catriona tried to reach Alain to ask what he'd unleashed upon them. He didn't answer. Next, she called Sean. When she was unable to hunt him down, she tried Luther.

"Hey Luther, have you seen Sean?"

"No."

"I wanted to let him know Tyler is on his way back. Commercial. Alain let him go with a warning. But the weird thing—"

Luther cut her short. "Okay, I'll let him know."

Catriona heard the line click dead and scowled at her phone.

"Well, that was borderline rude. He hung up on me."

Broch shrugged. "Ye dae tend tae prattle oan."

She gaped at him.

"I do *not*."

Twenty minutes later, the taxi pulled beside a large warehouse surrounded by desert. Catriona leaned toward the opening between themselves and the driver.

"I need you to wait for us."

The driver shook his head. "Nope. I have places to be."

"You could have told us that before you drove us out here."

"I'm not a mind reader. I didn't know you'd want me to wait."

Catriona huffed and pushed cash through a hole in the plastic separating the front and back of the car.

They'd barely closed the doors before the taxi drove away. Catriona stood with her hands on her hips, watching him go. Getting back downtown would be tough. Maybe they could catch a ride with a worker. She turned to Broch, who stood stuffing the vest into the waistband of his jeans. The scarf he'd already thrown around his neck.

Back to business.

"We need to get a feel for how this network is set up, so let me do the talking. I'm going to interview the foremen and the workers."

He rolled his eyes. "Aye. Ah ken my role."

"It's not that you can't be useful, it's the accent—"

"Aye. Aye. Ah'm juist here to crack skulls."

Broch released a deep sigh and Catriona could tell he was playing with her.

She tapped him on the chest. "I thought you were really hurt."

He smirked and put a hand on her cheek. "Ye kin dae a' the talking, my sweet little lassie. Ah'm juist 'ere tae support *ye.*"

She giggled and slapped his chest again. "Shut up. You've been watching too many women's talk shows."

There were three enormous, closed bay doors on the side of the building and one regular-sized entry. She turned the knob on the smallest portal and found it locked. There was a button next to the door and a camera mounted above, pointing at them.

Catriona pushed the button. "Hi, I was sent here by Mo?"

After a short delay, a voice crackled back at them "Name?"

"Catriona Phoenix."

She heard a buzzer and tried the knob again. The door opened. She looked up at Broch and found him staring off down the road they'd just traveled. She turned to follow his gaze.

Three cars sat parked on the main road at the end of the long drive leading to the warehouse. There were two sedans and one long black car, resembling a small limousine.

"I wonder who that is," she said.

"Aye. Me tae."

"It's probably a group leaving Vegas who needed to pull over to get their bearings."

She opened the door wider and ushered him in. With one last lingering stare at the parked vehicles, he followed her

Catriona and Broch picked their way past unorganized piles of boxes until they reached the center of the warehouse. A man sat at a table eating lunch from a brown paper bag. He looked up at them as another worker appeared from the opposite direction.

"You said Mo sent you?" said the approaching man as he raised his hand to shake.

"Yes. We need to ask you a few questions about the clothes being sent to burn—"

What sounded like a gunshot exploded behind them. The warehouse foreman jerked his hand from Catriona's grip to cover his head. Catriona felt Broch throw an arm over her as they ducked.

A flash caught Catriona's eye. A beam of light streamed across the floor from the now opened door. She remembered being buzzed in and knew the source of the bang.

Someone shot the lock open.

Footsteps headed in their direction. Catriona heard the intruders muttering and knew it was too late to run.

Two men rounded a stack of boxes, leading with semi-automatic rifles, screaming for hands to be raised. Walking at a measured pace behind them came the Slavic-faced man whose head had poked through the red beads at the Chinese restaurant.

Volkov.

Seems their reprieve from the Russian's hounding had been temporary.

"Her and him," he said, pointing to Catriona and Broch.

The two warehouse workers, one standing and one still cowering in front of his lunch, stared with wild eyes as two of the armed men ushered Catriona and Broch toward a wall of boxes marked *Modacious*.

When they were near the wall, Broch spun, his hand whipping out like a cobra strike. He grabbed the nose of the gunman's rifle and yanked it to the right side of his own body, jerking the man holding it toward him. Broch struck him square in the face as he stumbled forward. The man's momentum abruptly changed directions and he floundered back, his nose erupting with blood.

Broch had the weapon, but he couldn't turn it before one of Volkov's henchmen, a close-cropped blond man with a box-like build, lunged forward to grab Catriona's arm.

"Nope."

He raised his handgun to Catriona's head.

Broch looked at the gun he'd seized, and Catriona knew he didn't know how to use it. Not well enough to risk her life in the attempt.

"Drop it," said the blond.

Broch released the rifle. A third man stepped forward to strike Broch in the stomach with the butt of his rifle, pushing the Highlander toward the wall of boxes beside Catriona. Broch stumbled back, his eyes blazing with rage.

"What about these two?" asked a fourth henchman, his pistol trained on the warehouse workers.

Volkov stepped toward the man Catriona had taken for the manager.

"Is there anyone else here?"

Both men shook their heads.

Volkov turned to his soldier. "Take the bodies. Come back and take care of the cameras."

At the sound of the word *bodies*, the manager began to talk fast, the hands he held in the air, shaking.

"You don't have to kill us. We won't talk. We don't know anything. We don't know you."

Volkov smiled with only the right side of his mouth. "My name is Volkov." He gasped and covered his mouth with his hand, almost coquettishly. "Whoops. Now you know who I am. That is unfortunate. Now I'm afraid I don't have any choice."

The goon whose nose Broch had bloodied jerked the man from his lunch table seat and pushed him and the manager toward the door at gunpoint. He glanced back at Broch several times, making it clear he'd rather be walking the Highlander to his death.

The manager called over his shoulder as he headed toward the door.

"I don't even *remember*, man. I don't *remember* your name—"

Soon after they stepped outside, Catriona heard two quick pops.

The manager didn't speak again.

Volkov strolled to where Catriona and Broch stood.

"I suppose I owe you a thank you."

"How's that?" asked Catriona. Her voice couldn't summon

the punch she desired. She felt sick for the men who'd been walked to their death and sick that she and Broch would be next.

Volkov continued. "You gave me an idea. I've been waiting for the right time to cut out the middle man, and that time is now."

"We don't have anything to do with this—"

"I know. You're doing this for poor Mo."

Catriona heard a yelp and looked past Volkov to see Mo stumble into view, the man behind her urging her on with a pistol. He led her to stand beside them.

Mo looked at Catriona, her cheeks running with tears and mascara.

"What have you done?"

Catriona put her hand on her chest. "What have *I* done?"

Mo seemed both too furious and too scared to affect her French accent. With rising dread, Catriona realized she should have checked in with Mo after their ordeal in the Chinese restaurant. She'd assumed Volkov and Alain worked together and that Mo was safe.

Stupid.

But she wasn't going to take the blame for *this*.

Mo whirled to face Volkov. "What do you want? You're the one stealing my clothes?"

"Me? No. I *sell* them. Eastern Europe mostly. Many round women there." Volkov laughed and his men joined in, chuckling like a small private audience for his new standup routine.

Mo's lip trembled. Catriona couldn't tell if it was fury or fear.

Volkov sniffed. "Now all I need is the network of the man who *does* steal them."

Mo scowled. "What network?"

"It isn't only *your* clothes that he steals and I am not his only seller."

"And you think I know who this man is?"

Volkov laughed again, the curl of his lip revealing a gold-capped canine tooth. "Oh, you know him."

Mo shook her head. "If I knew him don't you think I would have had him arrested?"

Volkov took a step closer to Mo. "Who was the first person you called after asking these two to find the stealer of your clothes?"

Mo whispered the name Catriona already knew.

"Alain?"

Catriona had had her suspicions but hadn't wanted to believe it. Now, Alain letting Tyler go and asking her to leave without helping Mo made perfect sense. When she sounded doubtful about leaving, he'd sent Volkov to *scare* her into leaving, but Volkov changed his mind. He decided to cut Alain out of the equation.

Alain played a good little gangster, but it looked as if Volkov wasn't fooled.

Mo wiped at her eyes. "I don't understand. *What* about Alain?"

Catriona sighed. "He's selling your leftovers, Mo. He's using this creature to peddle them in Russia."

Volkov studied his nails. "Mostly Serbia. Some Russia."

Mo scowled. "Alain would never—"

Catriona touched her arm. "He would. It's what he does. He's a thief."

Mo's jaw fell slack. "He... From *me*? He's stealing from *me*?"

"You were leaving money on the table. What's a worse sin to a poker player?"

"But—"

"Enough!" barked Volkov. He motioned to Mo. "I'm taking you with me. The little Frenchman can have you back when he introduces me to his contacts and you both agree to give me your expired inventory."

Volkov strolled to Broch and tapped his shoulder with his handgun. "But not you. Alain didn't care much about what happened to you."

Broch remained expressionless, his eyes locked on Volkov's. His brazen stare seemed to amuse the Russian.

"You're not worried, big man?" asked Volkov.

Broch leaned forward. "'Tis ye wha shuid be worried."

Volkov chuckled and took a step back. He nodded to one of his men and glanced at the door. The man approached and motioned for Broch to move.

"No." Catriona tried to move but the square-bodied man beside her grabbed her hair to prevent it. Jerking her back into place, he raised his gun to her head to keep Broch from springing forward.

Catriona looked to Volkov, pleading. "He *is* important. Alain wants him alive."

Volkov shrugged. "I don't think so."

Broch headed for the door, the bloody-nosed henchman behind him prodding him with the tip of his rifle.

The Highlander glanced over his shoulder and smiled at Catriona.

"Ah'll find ye, lassie."

Catriona felt her eyes brim with tears.

He was nearing the door.

This isn't happening. This can't be real.

Catriona reached out to his retreating figure. She knew any movement could get her shot, but her arm swung out before she could stop it.

The man at her side flinched but didn't fire.

She called out.

"I love you, too!"

Broch crossed the threshold.

She swallowed.

I don't know if he heard me.

Catriona stopped breathing. It was as if her lungs had frozen in her chest. The silence in the warehouse throbbed in her ears as she turned to Volkov.

"Don't do it."

He shrugged. "It's done."

"It *isn't.* Don't do it. *Please.* You can have all the clothes. We'll never tell anyone—"

"You know that isn't true."

"It is. *It is true.* We'll go back where we came from and never—"

A *pop!* echoed from outside.

Catriona gasped. Legs buckling, she leaned against the wall and Mo caught her, holding her against her side.

"Oh, baby girl." She pressed Catriona's head into her bosom, holding her tight.

Catriona clung to Mo. "I never told him how much—"

"You did," said Mo, stroking her head. "He heard you."

CHAPTER FIFTEEN

The horse galloped on, proceeding as if it knew its destination. Sean clung to its back like a man strapped to a missile. He kept his eyes closed much of the time, opening them only to make small adjustments to the mare's trajectory.

There were too many things wrestling in his head for attention.

The image of a large truck rolled into his brain. He'd seen the vehicle in his rearview mirror. It had barreled toward Rune as the lanky bastard stumbled into the street, gun in hand.

He could see those skinny legs pumping. Sean remembered thinking Rune's pursuit of him was akin to being dogged by Ichabod Crane.

Then there was that moment—an almost giddy moment—when he knew the truck and his enemy had a date with destiny. The time for Rune to dodge the approaching vehicle had passed.

The truck struck him.

Rune flew into the air, arms and legs swinging akimbo, then...*nothing.*

He never landed. But then he was back.

Could I have missed seeing him land?

I missed it.

He'd looked away to be sure he wasn't driving off the road...

But I only looked away for a second.

He'd stopped the Jag in the middle of the road to watch the scene behind him in his rearview. The truck driver scrambled out of his cab. He, too, looked confused, searching for the man he'd struck. He probably hadn't seen his accidental victim land either. The trucker looked up and down the road, and Sean realized the man could see his Jag.

So Sean hit the gas and drove another fifty yards feeling confident the truck driver hadn't seen his license plate—and feeling *joyous* he wouldn't have to worry about Rune coming after Catriona or Broch. He crested a hill—

And there he was again.

Rune, standing in the middle of the road. One shoe missing, his white sock glaringly white in the California sun.

The man he'd watched struck by a truck behind him was now in front of him.

How?

How had he only lost a shoe?

Rune couldn't have been knocked three miles forward by the truck. He couldn't have flown through the air, landed on his feet, and raised his gun like some kind of gymnast sticking the landing.

But there he stood, like a bullfighter, daring the Jaguar to rush him.

The truck would have killed him or nearly killed—

Sean opened his eyes and watched the horse's hooves throw clumps of peat below him.

That was it.

The truck had *nearly* killed Rune. *The skeletal wretch had moved forward through time.* He'd used time travel to heal his snapped bones and crushed organs.

He'd been able to control where he was sent—how far away and how far in the future—*with precision.*

Sean felt a wave of envy wash over him. He'd hoped to teach Catriona and Broch what he knew of their heritage and abilities—and now he realized he knew *nothing.*

Gathering the reins in one hand, he wiped the mist and horsehair from his face, before closing his eyes again, squeezing them tight.

How did I fail in so many ways?

He had two young time travelers in his charge and he didn't understand his *own* powers. How could he teach them anything? Meanwhile, Catriona's real father was popping in and out of time like a person walking in and out of a room.

Catriona's *real* father bent time to his will.

Jealousy boiled in Sean's veins.

Not that it mattered now. He wasn't even in the same century as his children.

Amy Vansant

Sean's eyes opened again.

Rune is.

He'd almost missed the worst part.

For the short time he'd been able to dwell on the events of his strange day, he'd been running under the assumption Rune wanted revenge for the loss of his arm. But what if his revenge was incomplete? What if he wanted Catriona and Broch dead as well?

Sean felt his body slipping left and tightened his grip on the mane to right himself. He squeezed his thighs against the horseflesh.

I'm tired.

He couldn't stop. There was nothing he could do to help Broch and Catriona now. Today was his only chance to save *Isobel.*

Perhaps that was the key to helping the others.

If I save Isobel, it will change Broch's fate as well.

He could remain in Scotland with his wife and child. Then, maybe, when the boy grew older, they could find Catriona together. From what they'd been able to put together, she and Broch had met once before in ancient Scotland so she was *here*, or would be here, *somewhere*. They could find her and they could be together again, just not in Hollywood.

And there was hope for Catriona and Broch in Hollywood in the meantime. Luther was there. He'd protect them—his most loyal friend would go on alert when he showed up missing—though Sean cursed himself for not better prepping Luther for the event of his disappearance. When he'd confessed his time-traveling past to the big man back in the day, Luther had barely reacted. It was as if Sean had told him he was from Albania or Canada, not some other *century.*

Sean spotted a tree that felt familiar to him and adjusted the path of the horse.

I'm nearing home.

He was close. Memories of his time with Isobel flooded his synapses. Her hair, her eyes, the feel of her skin. He needed to get to the cottage in time, find a weapon, and be ready to fight off Thorn's men. He'd have to explain to his wife why he looked thirty years older than he had when she'd awoken beside him that morning, too. That wouldn't be easy. Maybe he could pretend to be his own long-lost uncle.

Hopefully, he could keep his wind long enough to defeat

the men determined to burn his home to the ground. Maybe he could remember how to use a sword. Swordplay wasn't a skill that came in handy in Los Angeles. The last time he'd used one was to cleave Rune in half.

Those were the days.

Sean spotted a thin trail of smoke rising into the air in front of him.

No. No no no...I can't be too late.

He spurred on the horse and the creature found a new gear, eating the ground with long strides.

As he and his mount crested the hill, he saw his cottage, flames already licking one side of the thatched roof.

Two men stood outside his door, holding it shut.

Laughing.

Sean felt his anger blaze, his brain buzzing like a hornet's nest. One of Thorn's men turned as he approached and tapped the other on the shoulder, pointing. The cowards abandoned the door and bolted to their horses. The thinner of the two leaped into the air as if spring-loaded, straddling his steed and galloping away from Sean's approach. The other man, more stocky, fumbled for the stirrup of his saddle, making one attempt to mount and then another.

Sean rode up beside him and jumped from his borrowed horse, forgetting his bones had aged since his last visit to Scotland.

The wind knocked out of him as he collided with the man and pulled him to the ground. Sean punched the would-be murderer in the side of his head. His knuckles screamed with pain but his blind rage prevented him from adjusting his aim toward softer flesh.

He struck again, landing two more blows to the man's temple. His foe's eyes shut and his head lolled on his neck. Sean scrambled to his feet, leaving the unconscious man behind.

"Isobel!"

He ran at the cottage, throwing his shoulder at the door. It gave way with little resistance. Smoke billowed outside as he plunged into the cloud, heading toward the outline of his wife on the ground. She lay on her stomach, hands stretched above her head, as she reached for the far corner of the room.

She looked up at him as he crouched below the worst of the smoke.

"Broch—"

Sean turned in the direction Isobel had been crawling. Broch lay on the bed in his swaddling clothes. The flames traveled along the back of the cottage wall. Any moment the bed would light like a tinder.

Sean scrambled to the straw mattress and snatched the boy into his arms, pressing him against his chest. Even in the smoky room, he could smell the sweet scent of the boy's soft hair. His head spun with memories of holding his newborn son.

The pride he'd felt.

Still crouching, Sean ran outside. He set Broch on the ground a safe distance from the fire and glanced toward where he'd left Thorn's man. The bastard and his horse were gone.

Good.

The craven wretch might have played possum or he might have awoken. It didn't matter now. There would be time later to hunt him and his friend like the dogs they were. For now, he didn't have to worry about the boy's safety.

Sean ran back inside the cottage and dropped to his knees beside Isobel.

He grabbed her hands and she pulled against him. "Broch—"

"He's safe." Sean coughed and again tried to gather her in his arms. His wife had rolled on her back since he'd left her. He saw her stomach was scarlet with blood. She'd been run through. The size of the wound—he didn't know how she'd survived a second after the blade left her flesh.

But I do know.

She'd needed to save Broch from the fire. She couldn't die until he was safe.

Isobel's lids fluttered open as he gripped her shoulders, preparing to drag her out.

She grabbed his arm.

"Ryft?"

He paused, stunned she had recognized him, calling him by a name he hadn't heard in so long. To hear it spoken in *her* voice, broke his heart.

She squeezed his hand and smiled before her features fell slack. Her grip on his fingers released.

"*Isobel.*"

Taking a deep breath, he grabbed her arms and stood, his head engulfed by smoke. He jerked her toward the door as a beam from the roof slipped, dumping the flaming thatch on him. He raised his arms, shielding Isobel with his body. The burning embers melted through his shirt, stinging his flesh like a swarm of angry wasps. Seized by a racking cough, he found it impossible to see through his watering eyes. He struggled to find his wife's arms again. Just as his fingertips located her flesh, something bumped into his back, blocking his path to the door.

"Leave her," said a low voice.

Sean ignored the man and gripped his wife's arms tighter. The heat intensified. A timber fell from the ceiling and landed where his boy had lain a moment before.

He was out of time.

The man slipped his hands under Sean's armpits and jerked him toward the door, forcing him to lose his grip on Isobel.

"No!"

Sean fought to break free but the man held him in a headlock, pulling him off his feet and dragging him toward the door. He thrashed, heels sliding across the floor, growing ever farther from the body of his wife.

"Stop!" he barked the words between coughs. His head swam, his breath coming in short insufficient gasps.

They crossed the threshold of the cottage and Sean felt his heels sink into the ground. The man dragged him another ten feet before dropping him to the dirt.

Sean rolled on his stomach and rose to his hands and knees, coughing, his nose clogged with ash.

He tried to speak but found it impossible.

"Stop trying to talk. Just breathe, man."

Sean twisted, trying to crawl back toward the house, eyes blinded by smoke and pain. The man pushed him with what felt like his foot, toppling him to his side.

"Catch your breath, you dumb bastard. She's dead. Stop already."

Sean shook his head, his chest heaving as he tried to breathe.

He heard the roof of the cottage give way behind him.

Too late.

He'd traveled nearly three hundred years for a second chance and he'd been *too late.*

Still blinded by tears and convulsions, he tried to scream at the man but the words caught in his throat.

Throwing out a hand, he squeezed a clump of peat in his

fingers and tried to claw his way toward the cottage.

"Sean. Stop."

Another racking cough made Sean curl as he fought for air.

He managed a gulp of breath and used it as a base for calming himself, pulling and pushing small sips of oxygen until his coughing subsided. Rocking to a sitting position, he watched his cottage engulfed by flames through squinted, watery eyes.

"Isobel," he whispered, not daring yet to speak in full voice. His lungs felt as if they were filled with attic insulation.

The man who'd pulled him from the fire crouched in front of him, wiping the soot from his eyes with enormous thumbs, even as Sean fought to stop him.

"Leave me alone," he croaked.

He pulled away, squinting until the man's head blocked the glow of the hazy sun, and his features melted into view.

Sean could only wheeze the name.

"Luther?"

CHAPTER SIXTEEN

Broch walked outside and paused to scan the surrounding area. Heat radiated from the parked cars in wavy lines, softening the edges of everything baking beneath the relentless desert sun.

He made a clicking noise with the corner of his mouth.

Whit a hell-scape this place is.

Devoid of life, the world around him throbbed like a wound.

He felt the tip of a rifle poke his back.

Lifeless, bit fer the eejit poking the gun intae mah ribs.

A trill ran through the muscles in his back, taut like the strings of a harp.

Ah'm goan tae enjoy this.

He took another step before the gunman poked the back of his arm. "Turn around."

Broch did as he was prompted. The man leaned his face closer.

"What are you smiling at, moron?"

Broch thrust his hands into his pockets and shrugged. "Ah'm a happy laddie."

The man spat. "If I were you I wouldn't be smiling."

Broch grinned a little more broadly and nodded to the building "She admitted she loues me. At the end there. Did ye hear it? Ah tellt her afore and now she's tellt me."

The man scoffed. "Lot of good that bitch's love is going to do you now. Take a look at your new home." He motioned behind Broch with the gun.

Broch turned to the van behind him and tilted his head to peer inside. The bodies of the two workers lay there, partially stacked on each other. Plastic lined the floor, as if the killers had always known the van would be used for transporting bodies.

Broch shook his head and mumbled. "Ye didnae hae tae kill them."

"What?"

With his head still turned toward the van, Broch took a step back, toward the gunman, mumbling a poem he recalled from schooling with his friend Gavin in Scotland.

"Come hither, hither, bonny fly, with the pearl 'n' silver wing—"

The ground behind him crunched as the gunman shifted forward to poke him again. "I can't understand a word you're saying—"

Broch knew the sound of crunching sand meant the man had stepped forward.

He dropped to a squat and spun, striking the side of the man's knee with the back of his curled fist. With a sucking *pop!*, the joint gave way. Above his head, the gun fired a single shot as the man yelped in pain.

The shot masked his cry and Broch kept his advantage. No reinforcements came running.

As the gunman folded to the ground like a faulty tent, Broch pounced, covering the murdering bastard's mouth with his hand. His crippled foe's arms flailed, clawing at Broch's neck, fighting to wrestle free. The Highlander flopped back to a sitting position on the ground, jerking the man's head into his lap.

The guard reached for a knife strapped to his thigh.

Cannae have that.

With a sharp twist, Broch turned the gunman's neck until he heard the muffled crack of his spine. The man fell limp in his arms. The knife and the hand wrapped around it fell to the sand.

Broch stood, allowing the man to slide from his lap to the dust. He wiped his hands and bent at the waist, grabbing the dead man by his shirt and pant leg. With a swinging heave, he lifted and tossed the lifeless body beside the workers in the van, sorry those unfortunate men would have to spend such intimate time with their killer.

He pressed shut the doors with a muffled click.

Broch picked up the gun and stared at the warehouse door, calculating his next move.

Inside, he heard voices growing louder.

Na time to plan. Someone's comin'.

Broch scrambled around the side of the van and pressed his

back against it, studying the gun to be sure this time he'd know how it worked. The design was a far cry from the pistols and shotguns he'd used back in Scotland and only vaguely similar to the handguns Catriona carried.

He wrote *learn how to use big guns* on his mental to-do list.

The nose of a black car rolled around the corner of the warehouse and Broch shifted toward the front of the van to find a better hiding spot. He poked his head far enough out to see Volkov exit the building. Another soldier led Catriona and Mo at gunpoint into the back of the long black car. Volkov entered behind them. The car seemed long to Broch, and he guessed quite a few people could fit into the back of it.

He looked at his stolen gun.

I cannae risk it.

To start firing an unfamiliar weapon at armed men when Catriona lay in danger's way, wasn't an option.

Frustrated, he flattened himself against the van as the black car rolled away, taking Catriona with it. Two more men had departed the building. The goons stood together, talking and smoking as if they were in no hurry to leave.

Broch moved back to the passenger side of the van. He eased his fingers under the latch and opened the door to crawl inside, doing his best to stay silent. Contorting his legs and back, he slid into the driver's seat and released the breath he'd been holding since opening the door.

He ran through a list in his head.

Turn the key.

He checked and found the key hanging in the ignition.

Sae that's guid.

He wrapped his fingers around the key.

"Hey, where's Gino?" said one of the men behind the van.

Time tae gae.

Broch turned the key.

"There he is."

Broch glanced in the side view mirror and caught the eye of one of the men. The man's expression puckered.

Na. Ah'm nae Gino.

Broch put the car into drive and stomped on the gas as the man behind him pointed.

"Hey, that's not Gino!" He threw down his cigarette and ran forward.

The van's wheels turned on the loose dirt and then caught,

propelling the van forward. Broch heard the henchman yelling as he wrestled the beast of a vehicle under control and tore away from them.

A gunshot perforated the back of the van as Broch ducked and swerved. The second, third and fourth missed, but he heard the clank of a fifth as it ripped through the back of the vehicle.

Broch made a wide U-turn. He'd have to drive past the men to get to the road.

What was it that Catriona liked to say in situations like this?

Bummer.

The word made him laugh.

Sliding toward the floor, he pointed the van at the men and pressed the pedal. Driving blind, he turned the wheel left and right, weaving toward them as they opened fire. The front of the van clanked with the sound of bullets riddling the engine.

He heard a meaty *thud.*

That wis nae bullet.

Broch peeked from his hiding place. Only the road lay ahead of him now. He glanced in the mirror and saw one man on the ground, the other leaning over him. Broch reasoned he'd clipped one. It was a lucky break. The remaining gunman was too busy helping his friend to fill the back of the van with additional bullets.

Broch raced down the dirt road leading to the main highway.

Ahead of him, the long black car had made its turn onto the asphalt. He followed, curving onto the street without pausing. He hoped to follow them to their destination and stayed back so they couldn't see it was *him* behind the wheel and not their hired hands.

His quarry drove a mile. Then the black car slowed and pulled to the side of the road to stop.

Broch slowed as well, remaining in the middle of the road.

Whyfur wid they dae that?

Two men stepped out of the back of the long car, guns drawn.

Shite.

Ah fergot aboot the infernal phones.

The men he'd left behind had no doubt called the men in the black car, warning them they'd lost the van.

Shite. Shite. Shite.

Broch slammed the van into reverse with a screeching of tires as a spray of bullets headed his way. He'd stopped far enough back that only a few reached their destination. He was grateful because he suspected the van's engine looked something like Swiss cheese. He didn't know very much about modern automobiles but felt sure only a miracle kept him moving.

Clear of the bullets' reach, he turned and roared in the opposite direction.

When the black car was nothing more than a dot on the horizon, he slowed the van to a halt, waiting to see if they came after him. They didn't. They didn't go back to pick up their men, either. They must have continued, headed for whatever place they'd always planned to go.

Broch ran both hands through his hair.

Whit dae ah dae noo?

He needed to go back. He needed to follow the long black car and find out where they were taking Catriona.

But that would be impossible. They'd know it was him. They'd shoot at him again, or worse, do something to harm the women. The last thing they would do is lead him to their hideout.

He squeezed his eyes shut, thinking. When he opened them again, he noticed a thin stream of smoke rising from the front of the van.

Och.

He didn't have long to get where he was going in the bullet-riddled van.

This is all Alain's fault. That wee French—

Broch's jaw creaked open as the clouds darkening his mind parted and the beam of an idea shone through.

That's it. It *was* all Alain's fault. He was the one who had called these men.

Alain knows them.

He needed to get back to Las Vegas and find Alain before the van died.

Broch pressed the gas and the thin stream of smoke escaping the front hatch billowed, pouring from the seals. The engine shuttered and shut off. Broch tried the key and the engine made a dry coughing noise.

Dead.

He dropped his head to the steering wheel.

Shite.

CHAPTER SEVENTEEN

Broch stood on the side of the road with his hands on his hips, staring across the desert landscape. The merciful sun had dimmed its glaring brilliance, and in the dying light, he saw the glow of Las Vegas in the distance.

But he was no fool.

Walking across the desert would be the death of him, sun or no sun. The terrain appeared treacherous and his throat already cracked with thirst.

Somewhere during the last hour he'd lost the phone Catriona had given him, so he had no way of calling the drivers who always came to his aid back in Los Angeles.

The black car with Catriona and Mo inside had headed in a direction parallel to the glow of Las Vegas, but he suspected the road curved toward the city soon enough. Broch reasoned Volkov had to be taking his hostages back to the city because he couldn't fathom people had built more than one town in the middle of the godforsaken sea of sand and rock surrounding him.

He walked in the direction the black car had driven. Best to put some distance between himself and the van with the three bodies inside. He didn't understand every law of the land, but Catriona had made it clear that killing people wasn't something to be taken lightly, even in self-defense.

In the heat of the moment, he'd forgotten that bit.

A thumping beat thrummed in Broch's chest.

My heart? Na...

Thumping music reached his ears. Turning, he spotted a car headed in his direction. The music grew louder as it neared.

Broch raised a hand and the car slowed, pulling to the side

of the road a few yards in front of him. As it passed, he saw the female driver's head-turning, as if she were arguing with other people in the car.

Broch jogged to the vehicle as the back window lowered and the music swelled louder. A jumble of screeching voices called to have the music turned down and it dropped until he could hear little more than the driving beat.

There were four middle-aged women in the back of the car staring at him, their eyes wild, teeth flashing as they giggled. Their faces were painted with more makeup than Catriona wore, but less than he saw on the actresses wandering around the studio lot every day.

"Hey there, sexy," said the woman in the back seat closest to him. She reached up and fingered the scarf dangling from his neck. "Need a ride?"

"Is that a Modacious scarf?" asked another woman.

"Why would he be wearing a Modacious scarf?" asked another.

The women's voices melted into giggles.

"Are you a stripper?" called the woman sitting in the passenger seat, her body twisting to better peer at him.

Broch recalled the billboard he'd seen of the scantily clad women. Catriona had referred to them as *strippers*. He glanced down to be sure his clothing hadn't shifted during his struggles. He appeared properly covered.

"Na. Ah'm nae a stripper. Ah dae need a ride—"

"Ooh! I volunteer!" yelped the girl farthest away from him in the backseat. The others hooted and held up plastic cups, clinking them together with a dull plastic tick, liquid sloshing.

"You're spilling!" scolded the driver.

"What's that accent?' asked the woman with short, blonde hair. She squinted at him as if she might be able to see his accent if she tried hard enough.

"Maybe he's from the Thunder Down Under," suggested her brunette friend.

A collective gasp echoed from the vehicle. "Are you Australian? Say *put another shrimp on the barbie*."

Broch smiled. Being told to say something reminded him of the game he played with Jeanie back at Parasol Pictures.

"Pat anither shrimp oan the barbie?"

The women squealed and the driver's window lowered. A dark-haired woman who looked as if she could be Catriona's older sister pushed down her sunglasses to peer at him.

"I apologize for them. They're a bunch of idiots." Her voice grew louder as she said the last sentence, and she dipped her head inside to be sure her friends heard it.

She returned her attention to Broch. "I'm the lucky designated driver. *They've* been drinking since two. Divorce party."

"I'm finally single!" screamed the brunette in the back.

The woman nodded toward the road behind her. "I saw what I guess is your van back about a mile? Run out of gas?"

Broch pictured the bullets riddling the front of the van. "Aye."

A hand reached out from the open back window, fingers curling around his bicep to squeeze it.

The driver scowled and turned to the back seat once more. "Stop molesting the man, will you?"

Giggles.

The music blared again for a moment before the driver threw out an arm and turned it back down.

She sighed. "I don't know how much longer I can control them."

"Are ye goan tae Las Vegas?"

"Where else do you think I'd be taking this band of idiots? Did you call for help?"

"Ah lost mah phone."

"Oh." She eyeballed him from head to toe and hooked her mouth to the side. "Tell you what. If you promise not to sue them for sexual harassment, you can hop in the back. If you dare. You'll die out here."

Broch looked in the back window and the women beckoned to him, daring him to get into the car. He looked down the long desert road, unsure which fate might be the most dangerous.

"Aye. Ah'd appreciate that."

The driver nodded. "Hop in. Don't let them push you around."

Cheers rose from the back of the car as he opened the door. As he dipped his head to crawl in, the brunette leaned over her friend to grab his scarf, whipping it off his neck and wrapping it around her own. The blonde shifted on top of her friend to make room and they slapped at each other for a moment as they fought for space. Once Broch sat and closed the door, the women collapsed, the closest to him landing on his lap.

She threw an arm around his neck.

"Hey there," she breathed, her face close to his.

Her breath lay heavy with booze.

CHAPTER EIGHTEEN

"Hey Sean."

Sean sat up and started coughing anew.

"Take it easy, man. Take your time."

Sean squeezed a word between each cough. His mind wrestled with the vision of Luther beside him.

This can't be happening. None of this can be happening.

"You let her die," he said in his staccato way.

Luther shook his head. "I didn't. You didn't either. Isobel was already dead."

"She wasn't...she..." Sean cut short and gasped for breath. His chest hurt in new ways, unrelated to the bullet hole in his chest. He felt as if he were going to drown in his own lungs.

Through blurry tears, Sean saw Luther thrust out a hand.

"We have to get out of here. Can you stand?"

"Can I—?" Sean twisted and spotted his son still wrapped in his swaddling clothes, one hand free and waving in the air.

"Brochan?"

"He stays."

"What? Lying there? That's—"

He felt Luther's enormous hands plant themselves, one on each of his cheeks, forcing him to face his old friend. His expression was as serious as Sean had ever seen.

"Listen to me, Sean. Isobel is dead. She died hundreds of years ago and there's no changing it. Broch will be found outside the cottage, just as he was always found outside the cottage. He'll grow up with the Broken Women and someday he'll find his way to you in Los Angeles."

"But—"

"There is no *but.*" Luther scanned the land behind Sean's

head. "Except we have to get our *butts* out of here before they come to find Broch. Before *you* come to find—" He moved a hand from Sean's face and motioned to the smoking cottage.

Sean found himself speechless. Luther lifted him by his armpits and he stood like an obedient child, his legs weak. They walked to his grazing, stolen horse, standing not far from the burning house, and Sean took the reins. Luther pulled them from his hands.

"Leave it. That horse wandered from home. You didn't ride it."

They walked a few steps farther to Luther's enormous steed. The white hair fringing around its hooves made Sean think of beer commercials.

Luther maneuvered him into place and helped him mount the horse. Taking shallow breaths, Sean allowed himself to be positioned again. He took his seat behind the saddle and Luther hoisted himself to sit in front of him.

"Hold on."

Sean turned to look at Broch, still happily waving at nothing, thirty feet from the remains of his mother and his ashen home.

"Are you sure—?"

Luther reached back to put a hand on his leg. "I'm sure. You know I wouldn't—"

"I know. You're the only one I would trust on this. But—"

"Hold on. I think I can let you watch."

Sean tightened his grip on his friend's waist and Luther spurred on his horse. The animal lurched forward and Sean squeezed with his legs to keep from sliding off the back.

They galloped for a few minutes before Luther reined in his mount. He lifted the gray, woolen cloak wrapped around his massive frame and glanced at his watch. "It's time."

He turned the Clydesdale to face the direction they'd come. Sean saw the cottage, the smoke barely visible now. From their position, tiny Broch was nothing more than a dot on the ground.

Sean felt bile rise in his throat.

I can't do this.

He was about to demand Luther return when a man and a woman appeared, running over the hill and into view. The man ran to the cottage and disappeared inside the sticks that remained. The woman covered her mouth as she watched. A moment later her head turned, as if someone had called her name. She scurried to Broch and picked him up. The boy must have cried, but Sean couldn't hear.

"My neighbors," said Sean, recognizing them. "They found him."

"I told you."

"So they're the ones who took Broch to the Broken Women?"

Luther nodded.

"They were poor. Another mouth to feed would have been too much." Sean tried to take a deeper breath and winced at the pain. He rested his forehead on Luther's shoulder.

"How did you know all this? What are you doing here?" he whispered, trying to avoid another coughing fit.

Luther reached down and patted the side of Sean's calf as he turned his mount. "We've got a lot to talk about, buddy."

Half an hour later, Sean sat across from Luther in a small dark tavern he remembered visiting thirty years previous, or three hundred years, depending on how he looked at it.

Across the room, he saw the booth where he and Isobel had supped during special meals out. It felt like only days ago, the way she'd picked at her lamb stew, pointing out the shameful lack of meat. They'd laughed about how much better *her* stew was, how maybe she should share her recipe with Luke, the tavern owner.

Feeling his emotion rising, Sean looked away and stared at the friend he'd only ever known in modern Los Angeles. He found it difficult to reconcile the image of Luther so misplaced in his old tavern. He still wore a gold earring in his left ear. He was still enormous, though the muscles usually visible peeking from the sleeves of his work polo shirts were now hidden by his large woolen cloak.

Sean took a deep breath, the sting of smoke still aching his lungs. He felt sadness on so many different levels he didn't know where to start or if he could muster the strength to begin.

"You made me leave my baby outside a burning building."

Luther grunted. "I let you watch the woman find him. I shouldn't have even done that. They could have seen us."

Sean put a hand on his forehead. "I must have knocked my brain in the car accident. This is some kind of fever dream."

Luther shook his head. "Not a dream."

Luke arrived tableside to place a tankard of ale in front of each of them. He eyed Sean's modern dress, frowning with suspicion. They made eye contact and Sean thought he saw a flash of recognition in the man's face. Just as quickly, Luke appeared to shake away the idea that he could be looking at a man he knew, thirty years older. He returned to his seat behind the bar with a grunt of disapproval.

Luther pushed the beer in front of Sean. Sean took a sip. It tasted real enough.

Luther raised his tankard and Sean spotted the collar of Luther's work polo beneath his cloak.

"You must have been in a hurry, too," he said.

Luther's brow furrowed and Sean pulled at his own polo collar to demonstrate what he'd noticed.

Luther's fingers scrambled inside the neck of his cloak to touch his modern dress. He chuckled.

"Yeah. Lucky, I knew where they were filming that dragon movie. Thought I'd grab a cloak to make life easier."

Sean looked down at his clothes. "I didn't have that luxury. So that white-eyed ghoul didn't get you too? He's not what sent you back here?"

Luther shook his head. "Not by his hand, anyway."

"So you *planned* this? How are you here? How did you find me? How did you never tell me—"

Luther held up a palm. "Easy. One at a time. I've got questions for you, too. We can take turns."

Sean scoffed. "Oh, by all means. Let's play a game. It's that kind of day."

Luther sniffed. "Tell me how you ended up here first. What happened to you?"

"Catriona's daddy happened to me."

"Rune."

Sean paused, his ale nearly to his lips, and put down the tankard.

"How did you know his name? Did Catriona tell you?"

"No."

"Then how do you know?"

"Same as I know your real name is Ryft."

Sean scowled, hearing that name twice in one day.

"I probably told you my name was Ryft when I first showed up."

"Yeah, well. I already knew it."

"So you knew this guy, Rune, back when I found Catriona? When I nearly cut him in half?"

Luther shrugged one shoulder. "Not exactly. I knew *of* him. Things were a little fuzzy that particular day."

"You got shot."

"Yeah, there was that." Luther took a sip and continued. "Rune came after you?"

Sean nodded. "He followed me from the lot. When I pulled over to confront him, he jumped from his car, gun blazing."

"He shot you?"

"Not just then. I dove back into the Jag and took off. In the rearview I watched a truck mow him down in the street. I was wondering how Catriona would take the news of her father being flattened when the bastard appeared *in front of* me, gun up and firing again."

Sean pulled down his shirt and showed Luther the angry red dent in his chest.

Luther winced. "Ouch."

"Yeah, *ouch*. I woke up here, pulled the bullet out of my lung, and..." Sean felt the pain of losing Isobel a second time intensifying and looked away to give himself a chance to check his emotions. "I thought I'd been given a second chance."

Luther shook his head. "Don't give that another thought. This was no second chance. You didn't screw up."

"It feels like it. And how the hell do you know? Why are you here?"

"I'm here for you."

Sean rolled his eyes. "I should have said *how* are you here. The Luther I know couldn't jump through time. Are you *God*? Was the Morgan Freeman portrayal closer to the truth than anyone knew?"

Luther laughed his deep baritone. "Naw, I ain't God."

"No. God probably wouldn't say *ain't*."

"He might."

"Fair enough. Who can say right?" Sean flicked at the bottom of his mug with his nail.

Luther sighed. "It took me months to train myself to say *ain't*. To blend in and be who I said I was. If I remember right, you didn't lose your accent overnight."

"Uh-huh. Help me out here. I'm trying hard not to *freak out*, as Catriona would say."

"No reason to freak out."

"Tell me *why*."

Luther tilted his head to the side, squinting one eye at his friend. "A lot of what's going on is on a need-to-know basis."

Sean felt a flash of anger. "Don't you dare tell me I don't need to *know*. I deserve some answers at this point."

"You do. You deserve a lot of 'em. And you're ready."

"Gosh, thanks."

Luther stared at the table and nodded his head slowly as if gathering his thoughts. "I got the call your car had been in an accident. But you weren't there and the tall skinny man the truck driver said he hit wasn't there either, so I had some idea one or both of you might have..."

Luther wiggled his fingers in the air as he raised his hand to imply flight.

"Flown away through time," said Sean, filling in the blank.

"Yup."

"Okay, I told you about my past, so I can see how you might come to that conclusion. But that doesn't explain how *you're* sitting here."

"No, it doesn't." Luther threw back the last of his ale and motioned to the man behind the bar for another. "There *is* somethin' I've been meanin' to tell you—"

Sean laughed and looked away, the insanity of the moment making it hard for him to concentrate. Or maybe it was the ale. He didn't know the alcohol content of ancient brews. It wasn't like there were labels. He only knew he felt *strange*.

He finished his pint and pushed it toward the end of the table.

Luke brought them two more tankards and took theirs away, blessing them with another distrustful glare. Sean's strange clothing and the ebony shade of Luther's skin would make it impossible for them to go anywhere without suspicious looks. Sean silently groaned at the idea of having to find scratchy wool replacements for his comfortable, one-hundred-percent cotton polo shirts. Modern-day had its perks and he'd come to expect them *all*.

Another random thought bounced through his head.

"*Catriona*. Did you—?"

Luther shook his head. "She doesn't know about you. She

and Broch are still in Las Vegas on the Tyler thing."

He nodded. "Good. I don't want her worried and I don't want her anywhere near Rune." Sean leaned back in the booth and took as deep a breath as he could, exhaling slowly.

Luther tapped the table with his finger. "That's what we need to talk about. You were never supposed to be here."

"No? Then why am I here?"

"Honestly? I think you wanted it so bad you made it happen."

"That's possible?"

"*I'm* here, ain't I?" Luther leaned back in his booth. "Remember Fiona told Catriona the two of them being together would help their father find them?"

Sean recalled the conversation. Luther had been eating a tuna fish sandwich when he relayed that information to him, and Sean thought he could smell the fishiness of it as he remembered.

"Yes..."

"She was right. She's young to know stuff like that, which worries me, because if you haven't figured it out, she's not on our side."

"*Our* side. Who are *we*?"

"The good guys."

"The ones who help people?"

Luther smiled. "You figured that out on your own."

"Sometimes I have half a brain," Sean muttered into his ale. He put down the tankard and looked up at Luther. "So that's how Rune jumped in front of my car? He just *wanted* to?"

"Yep. The truck put him on an unstoppable path toward death. So he left that time and started again, a few minutes later."

"In front of my car."

"Right where he wanted to be."

Sean straightened. "And I wanted to be *here*? To save Isobel?"

Luther nodded. "I suspect that's a big part of it. You didn't have any plan in mind so you followed your heart, literally."

"Is that wrong?"

"It's wrong to come back here. Anything you change could change everything in the future."

"So if I'd been able to save Isobel—"

"She might have had more children. Her children might

have married people that other people married in the world we know now. The disruptions are endless."

"So why was it so easy for me to pop back here?"

"Rune was near you. He tempted you to do something you shouldn't do. To follow your own selfish path."

"Because he's a bad guy. He and Fiona make people make the wrong choices."

"Exactly." Luther put his big paw on Sean's.

Sean thought about the things he'd done since arriving. The peasants he'd talked to—had he changed their lives by stopping them to chat? Then he'd stolen a horse and—

He gasped and looked up at Luther. "I saved Broch. He would have been in the house—"

Luther nodded. "It's a problem, but it's a problem that was supposed to happen."

"*Supposed to happen?*" Sean hit the table with the side of his fist, making the beers jump. "So you're saying my wife was *supposed* to die?"

Luther grimaced. "You know that ain't how I mean it—"

"Then how do you mean it? And how do you *know*?"

Luther put out a hand to rest it on Sean's. With his other hand, he pushed aside his ale and put a finger to his eye. He pulled down his lower lid.

"What the hell are you doing?"

Sean watched as Luther removed a contact.

"Since when do you wear—"

Luther looked up at him. His one eye was so blue it was nearly white. Sean had only ever seen eyes like that on one other person.

"Please don't tell me you're Rune's brother."

Luther laughed and replaced the contact. "Naw, you're too funny."

"So what does that mean?"

"Means Rune and I have been doing this for a long time. You ever notice your eyes getting lighter?"

Sean thought about it, picturing his image in his bathroom mirror at home.

"No."

Luther shrugged. "You're only on your third go-round. Just a kid, really..."

"My third—" Sean sighed. "Luther, I can't take much more of this today. Tell me what I have to do to get back home."

"That's easy." Luther grinned and raised his tankard. "You have to die."

CHAPTER NINETEEN

Catriona felt someone grab her roughly by the shoulder and pull her from Volkov's limousine. She pretended to stumble and rubbed her face on the man's arm as he tightened his grip and yanked her to her feet.

Her wrists were zip-tied behind her back. The plan had been to shift the blindfold over her eyes against the man's shoulder. Her scheme worked—at least well enough to peek out as she hung her head in apparent misery.

Not that she wasn't genuinely miserable. It had taken her most of the drive to control her emotions over Broch's assassination.

It all felt so stupid.

It had happened so fast.

One second he stood by her side and the next she watched helplessly as—

The car door behind her slammed.

Stop it. I can't think about him now or I'll be dead, too.

She hung her head and tried to get a picture of her surroundings. From what she could see through the crack in her blindfold, it looked as though they were in a neighborhood. Not a particularly nice one. Row after row of tan, stained-stucco ranch-style homes. Toys. Metal fences around the front yards with signs warning of dogs. The kind of neighborhood where people knew not to call the police about two blindfolded and bound women being led into a house.

People here kept to their business.

Luckily, the ball of fabric they'd shoved into her mouth shortly before stopping kept her from having to make the agonizing decision between *scream-for-help-and-be-killed* and *don't-scream-for-help-and-be-killed.*

Catriona tilted her head to get a better view of the house the men pulled her toward. This rancher looked like the others, except a man stood on the porch, looking as if he'd been expecting them. Tall, dirty-blond, coarse features, a bit of a paunch—the sort of face only youth made attractive for a brief moment in time. Hopefully, he had a wife or would soon. Time would not be this young man's friend.

The man at her side steered her with his grip on her upper arm. Her toe struck the first step to the porch and she lifted her foot to feel for the next riser. Impatient, the man dragged her up the next two and pushed her toward Paunchy.

"Put 'em in the room."

No sooner was the pressure on her arm released than it began anew, slightly lower, closer to her elbow, as the new man took over duties. He led her inside and she caught a brief glimpse of a sparsely furnished, depressing living room before being shoved unsuccessfully through a doorway. Her shoulder clipped the frame and she grunted in pain.

Catriona heard the sound of a jackknife opening and felt a rush of panic before the pressure began on the zip-ties around her hands.

They're cutting me loose.

Her hands sprang free and she reached up to pull the cloth from her mouth. She took a deep breath as she slid down the blindfold.

The door clicked shut behind her and she found herself in a windowless room lit only by a dull bulb in the light screwed to the ceiling. Fly-shaped shadows littered the bulb's opaque plastic enclosure.

Nice touch.

A blubbery cry brought her attention to Mo, the only thing keeping the room from being empty. The woman's muffled sobs had been the only sound in the car for miles and released from her gag too, she gasped in an attempt to catch her breath.

"It's okay, it's okay." Catriona took a step toward Mo and rubbed the woman's back with one hand.

It wasn't okay. There was nothing *okay* about their situation, but the only thing worse than being held captive was being held captive with a woman who couldn't stop crying.

"I don't understand what's going on," said Mo, sounding more defeated than panicked. It was a start.

"Your husband has been selling your leftover clothes to the Russians, or to Serbians, Albanians—whatever Eastern European hellhole these creeps crawled out of. That's what happened."

Mo squinted at her through already swollen eyes. "What?"

"It was *Alain*, Mo. You told him you'd sent me on an errand, didn't you?"

"Yes. I was mad he sent you to win me back, but you were going to help—"

"Alain didn't want me to solve your problem."

Mo tucked back her chin as if the concept of someone *not* wanting to please her struck her ears as foreign. "Why not?"

"Because *he's* the one who's been selling your clothes instead of burning them."

"Alain?"

Catriona rubbed her temples. She felt like she was talking in circles. "Yes."

"To *Russians*?"

Catriona sighed. The nationality of the heavies wasn't the information she'd hoped Mo would find troubling. "Sure. I dunno. Volkov has a bit of a Drago thing going."

"Drago?"

"The boxer. *Rocky Three.* Four? *Four.* It doesn't matter. He's got a touch of a Russian accent."

The corner of Catriona's mouth curled into a smile as she heard Broch's brogue in the back of her head.

Ye hae an accent. Nae me.

She shook her head.

Stop. No.

Somehow, Mo had wrapped her mind around her husband's betrayal and sat in stunned silence. Catriona moved away from her to rap on the walls. They sounded solid. Too solid for the inside of a house. Cement? It seemed this room had served as a prison before. She noticed a pattern of droplet-sized stains on one wall and scratched at one with her fingernail.

Dried blood, maybe.

Fantastic. That bodes well.

"Alain wouldn't do this."

"Ah, you're back." Catriona turned to Mo. "He would and he did."

Mo pressed her lips together, appearing to hover somewhere between rage and sadness. Despair won out and her eyes began to tear again.

Catriona tilted back her head. "I'm sorry. I didn't mean to snap at you. And I'm sorry to be the one to tell you—"

"It's okay." Mo's voice fell to a whisper. "I'm sorry about your friend."

Catriona opened her mouth and then shut it. She'd wondered if Broch's disappearance had penetrated Mo's shield of self-absorption.

Mo chewed on her lip. "He was your boyfriend?"

"It was complicated."

"It always is, right?"

Catriona nodded. "He wasn't stealing my clothes, but yes."

Mo chuckled. "I know, you're right. Alain is a thief at heart. I always did fall for the bad boys."

Catriona wasn't sure if five-foot-five Alain in his five hundred dollar shirts fit the *bad boy* mold, but she let it go as Mo barreled on.

"I should have known. I'm so sorry to have dragged you into whatever nasty scheme he's gotten himself into now. They're keeping me to hold over him..."

"Yep."

Mo frowned. "But why are they keeping you?"

Catriona's scalp tingled. Mo had struck on the dread she couldn't place, the phantom lurking in the back of her mind.

Why are they keeping me?

They'd had no problem killing Broch. They had to keep Mo for leverage over Alain. She'd been telling herself they thought she was also important to Alain, but why would they think that? Would Alain have said that?

Probably not. After all, he'd sent Volkov after them. So Volkov had to know she wasn't that close to Alain's heart—

Stop this line of thought...there be dragons. It's unproductive.

She flashed Mo a tight smile and wandered to the door.

Don't think about their reasons. Think about getting out.

She dropped to her knees to peek under the door but found it too close to the floor to see anything outside the room.

"I wish I could get a feel for how many people are babysitting us..." she mumbled.

"Do you think you can get us out of here?" asked Mo.

Catriona sat back. "I don't know. At some point, an opportunity might arise. We'll have to be ready."

"Peter, ask her where her husband is."

Catriona heard someone call from farther away. Maybe from out on the porch. The door rattled and she stepped back as the sound of a releasing padlock snapped. A moment later, Paunchy stuck his head in the door.

Paunchy Peter.

His attention locked on Mo.

"Where's your husband?"

Mo's hand fluttered to her chest. "What do you mean?"

Peter picked at the skin on his arm. "He isn't answering his phone and he isn't at your penthouse. Where is he?"

Mo shook her head. "I don't know. Did you tell him—?"

The boy scoffed. "Did we tell him we have you? *No.* That's what we're *trying* to do."

Mo's eyes widened. "I honestly don't know."

Peter opened the door to enter and Catriona stepped forward to block his path to Mo.

"She doesn't know."

He looked her up and down. "She knows."

Catriona looked into Peter's eyes. His pupils were dilated and jerky. That, combined with the way he itched and his general pallor, implied he had a drug problem. Meth-head if she had to guess. That was good. She didn't want a guard working at top capacity.

She wanted to escape.

Catriona motioned to Mo. "Why would she hide Alain from you? It doesn't help her. And why would she protect the man who's been lying to her? The man who's gotten her into this mess?"

Paunchy Pete hooked his mouth to the side and glanced at Mo, who raised her hand to her mouth and sobbed.

"*And* he's been cheating on me. I *hate* him."

Peter winced. It seemed she wasn't the only one finding the pitch of Mo's wailing unpleasant.

His jumpy eyes bounced in Catriona's direction.

"You better hope we find him soon."

She nodded. "If we think of anything you'll be the first to know."

She glanced at his hip and saw his gun there, tucked in his waistband.

Sloppy.

As Peter turned to leave, Catriona took a step forward, following him. He reacted, spinning to face her and blocking her path from the room.

She held up her hands. "I'm not trying to get out. I had a thought. Did you check Paris? He goes there a lot. The hotel, not the city. The restaurant...I forget the name."

The man grunted. "Get back."

She took a half-step back.

Paunchy Pete closed the door and she heard the combination lock snap back into place.

"Alain doesn't go to Paris," said Mo. "That would be so *not* him."

"I know. I wanted to get a peek outside. I didn't see anyone else."

"So he's the only one guarding us?"

"Maybe. It sounds like the people who brought us here are still out on the porch, but I'm thinking maybe they'll go."

She slid to a squat and put her ear against the door. "I'm going to listen for a bit. See if I can hear him talking to anyone."

Mo's shoulders slumped. "They took my purse. I need to fix my face." She licked her finger and rubbed through the river of mascara beneath her eye. "Where do you think Alain is?"

"He ran," said Catriona, wishing Mo would stop talking for a minute.

"He wouldn't leave me here. Would he?"

Catriona looked at her. "By now he probably knows Volkov is out of his league. I imagine he's...*confused*."

"That's a nice way of saying he left me to die, isn't it?"

Catriona shrugged. "Or he really might not know about you yet."

"I would hope not."

"But not long before I came to talk to you, he was busy carving words into the thigh of a twenty-year-old kid because he'd fallen behind on his bets."

"So?"

"*So* he's not a nice guy."

Mo shrugged. "The kid should have paid his bets."

Catriona chuckled. "You two are perfect together. He'd be crazy to leave you behind."

Mo smiled.

It was the first sign of hope her cellmate had shown. Catriona took it as an opportunity to motivate. "You need to get out of here, so you can kick that twisted little croissant's ass."

Mo's eyes flashed with the fire Catriona had always

associated with the woman. "You're right. I'm going to *kill* him."

Catriona smiled and put her ear back against the door, closing her eyes to listen. Her mind drifted to the image of Broch walking out of the warehouse, a gun at his back.

He turned to smile at her.

CHAPTER TWENTY

"We have to *die* to go back to LA?" Sean felt his expression fall slack. "You're kidding."

Luther clucked his tongue. "Nope. Not kidding."

Sean shifted back on his bench. His stomach didn't feel right. He could only imagine what bacteria might have been clinging to the side of his ale mug before the beer went in. "I don't know if I can stab myself in the neck. The firearms of this period are less than reliable. I could end up a vegetable in eighteenth-century Scotland for decades." He glanced at the tankard. "The food here might work faster."

"You ain't gonna have to stab yourself in the neck. I took care of it."

"Yeah? You brought a gun from home?"

"Not exactly."

Sean lifted his mug to his lips, smiling, strangely amused by the situation. Finding out he *could* go home had lightened his mood.

"There's already rope in Scotland so you wouldn't need to bring that. Poison...?" Before he could finish his thought, Sean knew the truth. He felt the blood drain from his face. "You said you *took* care of it. Past tense."

Luther nodded to the beer.

Sean dropped his mug two inches to the table with a bang, bottom-down, the contents jumping to splatter his face.

Luther guffawed.

"Come *on*." Sean wiped at his chin.

"It was in the first beer, so you can finish that one if you like."

Sean glared at the ale as if it were his enemy. "Thanks. I

wish I knew whether more beer would help or hinder the agonizing pain I'm no doubt about to suffer. Any insight?"

Luther shrugged. "Don't think it'll matter either way."

Sean looked back at the bartender. "What's Luke going to do when we start writhing around on the floor like we're possessed? We're going to scar the man for life."

"Good point." Luther finished his beer and stood. "Let's get out of here."

Sean glanced at his half-empty beer.

"Screw it."

He threw it back, gulping the contents and then smacked the tankard to the table. Standing, he followed Luther out the door. He raised a hand.

"See ya, Luke. It's been nice knowin' you. *Again.*"

Luke's permanent scowl ratcheted down another notch.

Sean followed Luther out the door. "You know, there are people here it might have been nice to visit before you killed me."

Luther glanced back at Sean. "Sure. I get it. Maybe you want to stay here? Catch up with the famine? Maybe give this guy a big wet kiss?"

Luther motioned to a man covered in a fine sheen of dirt, looking up at them from where he sat, his back against the side of the tavern. He had a festering wound traveling from the side of his mouth to the side of his nose. He smiled at them with blackened teeth and held out a hand. Luther dropped a coin into his palm from a safe distance.

"What was that? You brought money?"

"A quarter."

"How'd you pay Luke?"

"Tucked a twenty under my mug."

"Isn't that breaking some time rule?"

Luther shrugged. "We'll be dead by the time he realizes it and it will never make it to the future."

"The quarter might."

"Nope. I happen to know it doesn't. A seventeen-year-old kid drops it into the ocean fifty-two years from now."

"How could you possibly know that?"

Luther grinned.

They wandered around the back of the tavern and Sean felt the first real wave of pain crash against the walls of his stomach.

He burped and put his hand against the side of the building to steady himself. "I think I'm going to throw up."

"I wouldn't do that. If I go and you don't, let's just say it ain't as easy for me to get back here as you might think."

Sean felt another wave of nausea and fought to keep down his ale. "Exactly how much is this going to hurt?"

Luther shrugged. "Eh. You get used to it."

"You get *used* to it?"

When the third cramp tightened his insides like a knot, Sean's eyes rolled into the back of his head as he fell to his knees.

"I swear to god I'm going to fire you when we get back," he mumbled, scratching at the mud in agony.

He felt Luther lower himself to the ground beside him and take his hand.

"I'm right here with you, old friend."

Sean shook his head and spat the word again. *"Fired."*

Sean's eyes sprang open.

Drywall.

He stared at a white ceiling.

The corner of his mouth began to curl into a smile.

He wasn't dead. But at that moment, *dead* might have been preferable.

He felt as though a cadre of tiny insects marched up and down his cheeks. He could feel their sharp little feet, pinpricking his face. A chill ran through his body, but when he reached up to touch his forehead, he found it sweaty.

"Oh no."

He scrambled to his feet and ran to Luther's kitchen sink. As he hurled ale and froth into the sink, Luther appeared, nearly knocking him across the stove as he slid in beside him and vomited into the same sink. This set off a chain reaction and Sean once again emptied his stomach until the two of them stood hip-to-hip dry gagging.

Sean wrestled the spasm down and turned away from the sink, wiping his mouth. He heard Luther turn on the water.

"That's the most disgusting thing I've ever seen," croaked Sean. "And I just saw a guy dying of leprosy."

Luther scooped some water into his mouth, swished, and spat. Next, he splashed a little on his face and wiped it off away the kitchen towel hanging on the handle of the stove.

"Frat kids do this shit every weekend," said Luther.

Sean's stomach spasmed a final time as he rolled his hip along the countertop to rest his butt against it. He closed his eyes and took slow, easy breaths.

Luther walked away from the sink and let Sean take his place there. He removed the woolen cloak and draped it over his cheap wooden kitchen chair.

Sean rinsed the froth from his close-cropped beard and let his gaze wander the room. He never dreamed he'd be so happy to see Luther's crappy kitchen.

"Did I will myself here?" he asked, a little surprised he hadn't appeared in his own home.

Luther shrugged. "I helped."

"I felt you take my hand."

"Yup."

Sean sniffed. "You killed me."

"Yup."

"I only hope one day I get the chance to repay the favor."

Luther grinned, his deep, rich laugh filling the room.

CHAPTER TWENTY-ONE

"Back off the door. I've got a gun."

The return of Paunchy Pete.

His had been the only voice Catriona heard outside their prison's door over the hour they'd been locked in the little room. He seemed to be alone out there in the house. She'd heard him on the phone, presumably with a girlfriend. Someone who *needed to get off his back already.* He felt certain his *shit was under control.*

All riveting stuff.

At least Peter liked his meth. That could provide them with an opportunity.

Mo looked up from where she'd curled in the corner, picking at a loose hem in her tunic. Catriona reasoned the busywork kept the woman's mind off their situation, and for that, she was grateful. Keeping herself from spinning off into a blind panic was hard enough. She didn't know if she had the strength to soothe Mo with words of inspiration *she* didn't believe.

Catriona rubbed her palms on the sides of her thighs, readying herself to recognize and take advantage of any opportunity.

The doorknob rattled and Peter popped his head in to ensure they'd provided him with a clear path. Satisfied with their positions at the back of the room, he entered with a tray containing two paper plates slipped beneath two thin sandwiches. A pair of bottled waters completed the feast. He kept the tray balanced against his chest with one arm. The opposite hand held a pistol.

Catriona stepped forward to take the tray and Peter raised

the gun.

"Stay there."

Catriona stopped. "Sorry, Peter."

Peter had been lowering the tray to the ground, but he stopped as she spoke, his attention whipping in her direction. He straightened again, glaring.

Catriona smiled. "Oh, sorry. I didn't mean to be too familiar." She motioned to the world outside their door. "I heard you talking, earlier, to someone. They called you Peter."

He grimaced. "That's not anything you need to know."

"But I *do* know it. I can't un-know it. It doesn't matter. It's not like they're going to let me go and I'm going to run to the police screaming *Peter did it*. What good would that do?"

Peter scowled, clearly unhappy with the idea that she knew his name, but not *so* unhappy Catriona felt confident he knew they *would* be released.

She felt her smile falter.

They're not going to let us go.

She felt nerves flutter in the pit of her empty stomach. Sometimes a gift for reading people didn't tell you what you *wanted* to know.

Accepting his fate as a known entity, Peter lowered the tray to the floor.

"I have to go to the bathroom," said Catriona.

Mo perked, looking as if Catriona read her mind. "Me, too."

Peter's frown tightened another notch.

"Now?"

The women nodded.

He took a deep breath and sighed with a tone of resignation. "One at a time."

"Oh, I'll go first," said Mo.

Peter glanced at Catriona and she nodded.

"Let her go first."

Mo rocked forward and Catriona thrust out a hand to help her up.

Peter backed out of the room and motioned with the gun for Mo to follow him. He waved it once in Catriona's direction to be sure she understood to stay back. She considered rushing him, but he seemed determined to keep the gun pointed in her direction. Even strung-out, Peter was good at his job. His hands didn't even shake.

Maybe the girlfriend was wrong after all.

Peter closed the door and Catriona heard a bolt slide into place. The combination lock rattled and snapped shut.

Catriona stared at the closed door and then jumped up and down to get her blood moving, stretching her back with deep side bends.

It's now or never.

She couldn't keep hoping her chance would arise. She needed to *create* an opportunity. She'd be a fool to count on Alain coming through, and twice the fool to believe Volkov would let them go, even if Alain did everything he asked.

She picked one of the paper plates off the ground and smelled the sandwich, lifting the bread to inspect the contents. One piece of baloney split two slices of bright white bread. She didn't smell anything suspicious, but there were plenty of drugs and poisons undetectable by smell. Her stomach growled. She hadn't realized how hungry she was.

She put down the food. *Better not to chance it.*

The water seemed safer. The caps were tight and untampered with. She couldn't find any sign of leaking, or any hole possibly caused by an inserted syringe. No sign they might have resealed the cap. She cracked open the bottle, sniffed it and took a swig.

Tastes like water.

She gulped down the rest of the bottle. She could go longer without food but it would be unwise to grow dehydrated.

"Get back."

The door rattled again and Mo entered looking more relaxed. She'd taken the time to clear the mascara streaks from her cheeks, though her eyes remained swollen and red. She glanced at Catriona but didn't appear to possess any new information.

As she passed, Catriona whispered to her. "Anyone else out there?"

Mo appeared frightened to be asked. She slid to her seat in the corner and shook her head without looking at Catriona again.

"Let's go," said Peter, motioning to Catriona. The look on his face struck her as odd. No longer perturbed over the reveal of his name, now he looked at her with...*pity*?

He looked away. As if it pained him to consider her.

Catriona swallowed.

What does he know? Does he know why they're keeping me?

The moment Peter turned his head, his gun began to lower. Panic growing, Catriona pushed away the fear by kicking the weapon from his hand.

She hadn't planned it.

The gun clattered against the wall and skid somewhere behind the open door.

Mo screamed, covering her head.

Peter jerked back his hand, grimacing in pain, and then moved for the gun. Though she'd caught herself off-guard by kicking at the gun, Catriona *had* counted on him diving for the weapon. Only sheer will kept her from doing the same thing.

She remained standing, arms quivering at her sides with restraint.

As Peter's head dipped, she kicked him hard in the face.

Peter straightened like a bloom searching for the sun and then stumbled back against the wall, his nose streaming blood. His eyes locked on hers. Springing off the wall like a spider, he roared, charging at her. He led with his fist and Catriona used his momentum to deflect the punch. He caught only the edge of her arm and flattened against the wall, catching himself with his other arm before his head could hit.

Jumping on his back, Catriona wrapped her arms around his throat. Leaning back, she put the full weight of her body on his windpipe as he thrashed to break free, bouncing, pinball-like off the walls.

Mo squealed, doing her best to stay out of the way as they crashed around the room. Peter slammed Catriona against every wall, growing increasingly desperate to dislodge her. She clung to him like a bronco rider.

"Get out. Run!" Catriona screamed as her spine struck another wall and the wind pushed from her lungs.

Mo tried to move to the door, but Peter crossed her path, blocking her. As Catriona and her captor twirled like copulating dogs in the opposite direction, Peter finally fell to his knees. He hovered there a moment and then face-planted to the floor, unconscious.

Catriona held on a little longer. She could feel Mo in the room beside her and turned her head to confirm it. Catriona grimaced. She wanted the woman out before she let Peter loose, just in case he was playing possum.

"Go—"

She looked up and saw Mo staring at something in the

doorway. Catriona followed her attention to the hard man who had done all the talking at the warehouse.

The man who had cornered them in the Chinese kitchen.

Volkov.

Volkov reached out and grabbed Mo by her hair. She yelped and held up her hands, begging him to let go as he pulled her head down and toward him. With his other hand, he raised a gun to Mo's temple, glaring at Catriona, a maniacal glint in his eye.

"You like to fight?"

Catriona jerked against Peter's throat. "I'll kill your man."

Volkov laughed. "I don't even know his name. Plus, I'll shoot her and you before you can finish him."

Catriona grimaced. Her leverage on Peter's throat was the only leverage she had, and it was no advantage over Volkov's weapon. The gun behind the door was too far away to be of any help.

She slid her arm out from under Peter and sat up, still straddling his lower back. "Don't take it out on her. I was the one. She didn't do anything."

Volkov smiled. "I love your fire."

Unnerved by Volkov's wolfish leer, Catriona stood. Volkov motioned to her with the gun.

"Move to the corner."

She did as she was told. Volkov dragged a whimpering Mo closer to Peter's still form and kicked the boy in the ribs.

Peter groaned. Volkov kicked him again.

"Get up."

Peter looked up, bleary-eyed and sputtering. He raised himself to a sitting position and glared at Catriona, rubbing his throat as he tried to catch his breath.

Volkov tapped Peter's knee with his boot. "Hey. What did she do to you?"

Peter coughed his response. "What?"

"How did she get the better of you?"

Peter grimaced, still struggling to breathe. "She sucker-punched me—kicked—"

"She kicked you?"

Peter nodded, his eyes rolling in the direction of the gun still lying behind the door. Volkov followed his attention. He clucked his tongue in disapproval.

Peter knew his mistake had been spotted and his voice

grew whiney. "She kicked my hand—"

Volkov cut him short by shoving Mo at him. She stumbled and Peter raised his hands to block her from falling on him. Mo twisted, trying to disentangle herself from his flailing arms, and then landed hard on her ample rear end with an expelling of breath. She slid into her familiar corner looking equal parts mortified and frightened.

Volkov backed until he could retrieve Peter's pistol from behind the door, his gun pointed at Catriona.

"Would you say she's a kickboxer?" Volkov asked, throwing the gun at Peter.

He bobbled the weapon and then secured it, taking a moment to stare at it as if he expected it to leap from his hands again.

"A kickboxer?" he asked.

Volkov rolled his eyes. "Would you say she's a kickboxer? Or did she just *happen* to kick you? Was there skill in what she did?"

"I—" Catriona tried to interrupt. Volkov's obsession with her fighting style made her uneasy.

Volkov's eyes flashed in her direction as he raised his finger to shush her. His annoyance seemed so deep and genuine, words failed her and she fell silent like a scolded little girl.

Volkov turned his attention back to Peter.

"Maybe in her heart she is more of a street fighter?"

Peter's eyebrows slanted like an opening bridge and he stammered. "I, I don't know, she just...I didn't see..."

Volkov's disappointment in Peter's inability to describe Catriona's attack felt like an entire other being in the room.

He looked to Catriona.

"It feels unfair to ask, but are you a boxer?"

Unfair?

Catriona didn't understand Volkov's interest. At first, she'd thought he was performing a little play for his amusement. She'd guessed the final act would be the utter humiliation of Peter for being bested by a woman. But now, he appeared to have lost all interest in Peter.

"No."

"A kickboxer?"

Is he looking to hire me?

Catriona shook her head again.

"...No." She stiffened. She hadn't meant to pause but she

could see Volkov saw the lie.

He smiled, nodding his approval. "You *are* a kickboxer. Very good."

He kicked Peter's thigh, this time much harder. "Get up. Get out of here. You are useless."

Peter stood and with a last smoldering glare at Catriona, left the room. Volkov lowered his gun and, instead, pointed a tightlipped smile at Catriona.

"Good," he muttered once more before leaving and shutting the door behind him.

Mo's hand shot to her mouth to stifle a sob. "Why did you do that?" she asked from behind her quivering fingers.

Catriona leaned against the wall and rubbed her arm where Peter had clipped her. "I was trying to save us."

"You just made him madder. You almost got me shot."

"That part might be inevitable."

Mo glared at her. "Alain will save *me*."

Catriona tucked back her head, struck by Mo's vitriol.

Ouch. There it is again. *My expendability shoved in my face.*

She took a step toward Mo. "You're so confident Alain will save you? Where is he then? Your gangster-wannabee husband?"

Mo crossed her arms against her chest and looked away. "He'll give them what he has to."

Catriona grunted and moved to the opposite corner to sit. "Well, I'm sorry. I'm not going to sit in this cell and wait to die."

CHAPTER TWENTY-TWO

Broch and the party women arrived at Gold, singing a Scottish drinking song he'd taught them along the way. At some point, he'd been able to convey to the designated driver the name of the hotel where he wanted to be left and she'd been gracious enough to roll him to the door.

"Thank ye fer yer help," he said to the driver as they came to a stop at the doors of Gold.

She looked at him through the rearview mirror and rolled her eyes. "Thank *you*. You kept them distracted for me so I could concentrate on driving for two seconds."

The blonde on his lap had fallen asleep on his chest and he eased her back to the others as he slipped out from beneath her to a rousing chorus of goodbyes.

With a final wave of thanks, Broch entered the lobby and walked directly to the elevator. He rode it to the level beneath Alain's penthouse planning to climb the last flight. As the great metal box rose, he tapped the keyhole next to the button for the penthouse, remembering how Catriona had.

He'd thrown himself into singing with the women during his ride to keep from freezing in fear for Catriona. Left alone in the elevator, he could feel his anxiety looming, tapping on his shoulder, whispering in his ear that he'd never find her. Telling her the things that would happen to her when he failed.

Na.

Hold the anger.

He needed to stay sharp. Fear couldn't help Catriona. Dread and regret would only drag him down.

He pounded again on the door to Alain's level.

Philip had his gun drawn when he opened the door to the

stairwell, making it clear he had no intention of falling for the same trick twice. An angry red knot bulged on his forehead where Broch had smacked his skull into the ground.

Philip pointed his gun at Broch and shook his head. "No way, man."

Broch raised his hands. "Ah need tae talk tae Alain."

"No way. We sent the boy home—"

"It's aboot Mo. She's been taken."

Ripples rose on Philip's forehead. "Taken?"

"Taken. By bad men."

Philip lowered his weapon and sighed through his nose, his jaw clenching.

"Fine. Follow me, but no funny stuff."

Broch followed him to Alain's door, where Philip knocked and Dez answered. She seemed surprised and not overjoyed to see him.

"What do you want?" She tilted to look past him at Broch. "Have you lost your mind letting him in again?"

Philip grimaced. "He said something happened to Mo."

Dez scowled as she returned her attention to the Highlander, but Broch thought he saw a flash of surprise in her expression.

"Where's your bitch?" she asked.

Now it was Broch's turn to frown. "Ah'm goan tae let that gae. Where's Alain?"

"Alain isn't feeling well—"

A whisper hissed from somewhere behind Dez. "Ees that the Scot?"

Broch pushed the door. Dez attempted to keep it closed, wrestling against his weight, but he continued to apply pressure until it snapped from her grip. The door swung open to reveal Alain standing in the living room surrounded by suitcases. He looked pale and shaken.

"They hae Catriona and Mo," said Broch. He wasn't sure what reaction he expected, but something about the man's blanching pallor led him to believe the Frenchman already knew his wife's abduction was at least a possibility. Judging by the luggage, maybe he knew and didn't want to be next.

Alain shot an angry look at Philip and waved him away. "Go outside. Don't let anyone else up here, you filthy animal."

Philip grumbled and shut the door.

Dez stepped back and wrapped her arms across her chest,

her lips squeezed into a tight knot.

"Volkov took Catriona, too?" she asked.

"Aye."

She grunted and glared at Alain. The Frenchmen refused to look at her.

Broch turned his attention to Alain, who had collapsed into his chair like a throw draped across it.

"I suppose you're going to say this is all my fault."

Broch nodded. "Aye. Thit's why ah'm here."

"Weren't you with zem?"

"Howfur dae ye ken that?"

Alain shifted in his seat. "Why wouldn't you be with Catriona?"

Broch resisted the urge to choke the life out of Alain. It seemed Volkov had been in touch with the wee toad, and the coward's response had been to pack up and run.

"Aye, ah was there. Ah got away, but ah need tae find where they took them. Dae ye ken?"

Alain covered his mouth and pulled at his chin. "I sink I do, but zere's no way..." Alain put his hands on the back of his head and dipped his nose toward his knees as if he thought making himself small enough would hide him from his troubles.

Broch moved forward and took a seat in the chair opposite Alain. He needed to keep the man focused. If Alain fell apart now they'd be dead in twenty-four hours.

"Look at me."

Alain peered up, white ringing the bottom of his eyes.

"Tell me whaur they are. Tell me whit they want."

Alain took a deep breath and leaned back into the sofa.

"He's a Russian. I made a deal with him. I steal Mo's designer clothes and he sells zem far away. I built a network of bribery, thieves, fences—eet ran like clockwork. But Volkov wants to cut me out. He wants me to give him my sources and zen he will free my Mo."

"And Catriona?"

Alain glanced away. He was nodding but didn't look convinced.

Broch knew the man had no intention of securing Catriona's safety. Alain had already sent Volkov after them once. Only the Russian's greed had stopped him from killing them at the Chinese restaurant.

He leaned on his elbows and brought his face closer to

Alain's.

"Sae give him whit he wants."

Alain scoffed. "I wish eet were zat easy. He threatened me but I didn't listen. I know him better now. Once he has ze sources, he'll kill ze girls and me as well. He can't risk letting me live. I would know all his secrets. I could sever his connections to my people."

"Bit if he murdured Mo, he wouldn't hae her claes."

Alain sniffed and thrust out his boney chest. "Mo's clothes are a very small part of ze full operation now."

Alain's brag didn't impress Broch. Everything about the man felt smalltime. He'd never be in a position to take on the Russian. Not later and, unfortunately, not now.

He flopped back in his chair. "Yer a wee greedy shite, Alain."

Alain nodded. "It's true."

"Ye sent Volkov after us. Ah should wring yer scrawny neck."

Alain's eyes flicked in the direction of Dez.

"You're going to let him talk to me like ziss?"

Dez nodded. "I think I am this time. You knew about Mo and you were going to *run*?"

Alain shook his head and muttered. "I wouldn't be any good to her dead. I needed time to sink."

Broch raised a hand. "Och, dinna worry yerself. Ah willnae kill ye fer noo. Ah need tae find Catriona and Mo. Ye kin hang fer all ah care."

"Find zem? You're going to go after zem?"

"O' coorse ah'm gaun after thaim. Bit ahm needin' ye tae tell me whaur thay *took* thaim."

Alain stood and began to pace the room, pulling at his lips as if in thought.

"Oui. Oui...He has a place. Eet's a few miles off ze strip. A safe house."

"I know it," said Dez.

Alain looked at her. "You do?"

She nodded, looking grim.

Alain sighed. "I need to Volkov him my network."

Broch stood and pointed at him. "Yer nae goan tae dae a thing."

"I must. He's going to call back. I have to tell him."

Broch stepped forward, his jaw clenching. "Ye juist *tellt* me if ye gave him the information they'd kill Catriona and Mo."

Alain rolled his eyes "Oui."

"Sae *dinnae tell them*. As long as ye hae the information he needs, he cannae kill them."

"He could tahrture hair. I've heard terreeble sings ahbout ze mahn."

"He'll come keekin fur ye. Don't be home. They'll call yer phone. Don't answer. If he cannae reach ye he cannae threaten ye. Delay them. Gimme time tae git them."

Alain pressed his knuckles to his lips. "Fine. I can delay him for maybe twenty-four hours. After zat—"

Broch sniffed. "It wull be ower by then." He glanced toward the door and made a decision.

"And ah'm takin' Dez."

Alain straightened, his eyes wide. "What's zat?"

"Ah'm takin' Dez. She's goan with me."

Alain shook his head. "No. Take Philip. Dez needs to stay with me."

Broch grabbed the Frenchman by his shirt and jacket, lifting him to his toes. Alain let out a whoop of fear.

"Ah'm takin' Dez wit' yer blessings."

Alain nodded.

Broch dropped him to the ground and strode to the door to open it. He looked back at Dez.

"Yer with me."

Dez nodded and followed.

Alain attempted to protest but sputtered only air. Dez held up a palm.

"Save it. I'm doing this for her." She nodded once to Broch. "Let's go. I know the address."

Philip peered in the door. "Do you want *me* to go?"

"No." Dez and Broch said the word in unison.

Dez disappeared into the back of the apartment and reappeared with a pistol, which she slid into the back of her pants and covered with a light jacket. Without pausing, she passed Alain and Broch and left the apartment to press the elevator button in the hall.

Without looking at Alain, Broch followed, entering the elevator as the doors opened

Dez and Broch stood beside each other as the doors slid shut.

"He's not as tough as he pretends to be," said Dez.

Broch scoffed. "Ah ken."

"Mo's tougher."

"Ah believe that as well."

She looked at him. "I don't know Catriona well, but I know she's tougher than all of them."

Broch felt a wave of emotion crash against the back of his eyes and he sniffed, looking away to hide the tears welling there.

"Aye."

When the doors opened again in the lobby, Broch strode to the front desk.

"What are you doing?" asked Dez, jogging to keep up.

"Ah'm needin' tae grab something."

Broch dug in his pocket for his luggage ticket and claimed his bag. He opened it on the floor and pulled out his kilt, sporran bag and a sheathed knife.

"Jeezus, don't let them see the knife," said Dez stepping between him and the deskman's line of sight.

Broch kicked off his shoes and began to unbutton his jeans.

"You can't get changed in the lobby," hissed Dez.

He wrapped the kilt around his middle and dropped his jeans. Taking a moment to adjust the fabric, he attached his sporran and knife to his side. He pulled his leather boots from the bag and jerked them on.

Stuffing his jeans back into the bag, he zipped it and handed it back to the man. The desk clerk showed no sign of shock.

Dez shook her head. "Lucky for you we're in Vegas. I'm sure that's not even *close* to the weirdest thing they've seen today."

Feeling complete, Broch huffed a quick deep breath and pounded himself once on the chest with both hands.

"If ah'm goan tae dae this, ah'm goan tae dae it right."

He headed for the door and noticed his friend the magician. The mime's eyebrows rose with recognition.

Broch raised a palm to stop his approach.

"Ah'm sorry, wizard. Ah cannae enjoy yer magic balls nae."

Dez snorted a laugh.

CHAPTER TWENTY-THREE

"It's not that I don't—that I *didn't*—have feelings for him. It just all happened so fast. You know? He wasn't in my life and then he was waaay too much in my life. I think I resisted because of the timing, but seriously, who asks you to marry them after a month? But, there's something about him—I could feel it from day *one*. It felt like we'd always been together—"

Catriona heard a snort. She stopped mid-sentence to turn from where she'd been staring at the floor, deep in some kind of verbal trance.

Mo was asleep.

She sighed. Mo had asked her about Broch and she'd rambled through three months of sexual tension and giddy infatuation.

She couldn't blame Mo for nodding off. It had been a long, rough day for a pampered, sixty-year-old fashion designer. Catriona found the woman's light snoring preferable to the sobbing and complaining preceding it.

While Mo slept, Catriona stood and paced the room, listening at the door for sounds of life. The house had grown quiet since Volkov's departure from their cell.

She'd run out of escape ideas. The room had no windows. No opportunities. It was small and square and devoid of features that weren't a wall, floor, or ceiling. Even prison cells had *beds*. Where they'd been stored was more like an unfinished walk-in closet.

Maybe she could stand on Mo's back and reach the light screwed to the ceiling. Pull the dying bulb from there, and break it into a makeshift knife...

She chuckled at the idea of telling Mo she needed her to be a stepstool.

They had no tools other than two paper plates and a half-uneaten sandwich. Mo had eaten her lunch. When she was finished, Catriona quizzed her about her stomach, mind, and overall health. She'd seemed fine. Fine enough that she'd gone on to eat half of Catriona's sandwich. Now, she slept like a baloney-filled baby. It could be something in the food making her sleepy, but there was no reason to think the woman wasn't just *exhausted*.

Or bored with the Highlander romance that almost was.

Catriona leaned her back against the wall and slid to the floor. The memory of Broch attempting to dirty dance for her after he'd watched *Magic Mike* cha-cha'd through her mind.

She smiled.

Where was Kilty now? Had he woken up a few years in the future, healed by time travel? Or had he been reborn as an infant, as she had, maybe hundreds of years in the future, ready to start life anew?

Maybe he went *back* in time. Maybe he was somewhere nearby, ten years older.

Or ten years old.

Awkward.

She didn't know what realities were possible.

A wave of regret built until she felt her chest tighten. Catriona closed her eyes, wiping them dry, trying to erect an emotional breakwater to stop the rising tide. She'd have the rest of her life to think about what might have been. *Hopefully.* Right now, she had to get herself out of the Russian's grasp before he sold her to some human-trafficking kickboxing syndicate or *whatever* he was plotting during their last strange encounter.

Outside the door, she heard the padlock snap. She stood.

The door creaked open, the light from the living room appearing like a bright slice of pie on the ground.

Boy, I'm hungry.

The silhouette of a man appeared in the doorway. It took Catriona's eyes a moment to adjust, but as the figure's features came into focus, she found they weren't as half as interesting as his clothing choice.

Volkov wore a short, shiny red robe. The sort she'd only ever seen on boxers and television soap opera temptresses.

The Russian's legs and feet were bare. Before she could react, something struck her chest like lightning. She braced herself to keep from falling back and then dropped to her knees as pain radiated through her torso. Her limbs went numb.

Stun gun.

She'd felt the sensation before. Sean had tazed her once during a training session. She hadn't liked it then either.

Catriona collapsed forward on all fours. At the sound of her striking the floorboards, Mo awakened with a surprised yelp, scrambling against the wall already at her back.

Volkov strode in and zip-tied Catriona's feet and hands as if he were a cowboy and she a prized calf. He shoved a cloth into her mouth.

Limbs paralyzed, she couldn't stop him.

He hefted her over his shoulder and pounded out of the room, leaving the door behind him open as he carried her through the living room and into a kitchen littered with dirty dishes.

Paunchy Pete keeps a poor house.

What a dumb thing to think.

I'm trying not to think about what's happening to me.

Catriona felt the sensation in her limbs returning. She thrashed as he moved through the kitchen and into an enclosed porch off the back of the house. She could feel the cold of the desert evening seeping through the flimsy walls.

Twisting, she slipped from his shoulder. She believed she'd thrown him off balance as she fell, but soon realized he'd simply dropped her on purpose, like a bag of grain.

Spinning on his heel, Volkov returned to the living room. Catriona heard the door to her former prison close. No reason to lock the door if the room was empty.

Mo didn't run.

Catriona rolled toward a door leading outside. She kicked at it and caught a quick glimpse of the backyard twice before Volkov returned. The door had been flimsy enough to bend but secured by a latch near the top. A peek of freedom would be all she saw.

Volkov grabbed her by the hair and dragged her into the middle of the room. She felt a clump rip from her scalp and screamed, the sound muffled behind the rag in her mouth.

Releasing her, Volkov moved a wicker sofa away from the outer wall and opened a hatch in the floor where it had sat. He lifted Catriona by her armpits and, straddling the square hole in the floor, dangled her over it.

Straining to see through the darkness below her, Catriona struggled to keep her bound feet from threading through the hole beneath her. She saw no bottom. Her panic grew.

Volkov dropped her into the darkness.

Weightless and blind, Catriona's mind blanked white with the fear she'd fall forever or into some dank well.

She'd never been so happy to clip her shoulder on something.

A moment later she was on the ground. She'd landed awkwardly and fallen to her side on what felt like a padded mat. She could only think of one reason the floor would be padded.

He's done this before. He's dropped someone down this hole before.

It was a *thing*.

She heard the hatch close, and the already dim room plunged into total darkness. A second later the mat bounced beside her.

He's in here.

Light flooded the room, so fast and harshly Catriona felt her pupils contract. She squinted and blinked hard, giving her eyes a second to adjust, but also trying to *see* everything she could.

The ladder she'd clipped on the way down appeared bolted to the rough, red stone walls. Blue wrestling mats covered the floor around her. Volkov stood to the left of the ladder next to an industrial-looking electrical box, hunched, unable to stand beneath the low ceiling. He looked down at her and smiled to find her watching him.

Without thinking, Catriona rolled in the direction she felt gravity tugging. It meant heading deeper into the underground bunker, but it also took her farther from Volkov. The urge to stay away from him conquered all other urges.

The floor slanted like a ramp, leading her into a larger and taller chamber. She flipped, three times, feeling like a fish on a hook.

Without the advantage of the ramp, progress stopped once Catriona entered the large chamber. Bunching and releasing like an inchworm, she dragged herself toward one of two archways on the opposite side of the room, hoping one of them contained another way out. Blue mats lined both the floors and the lower half of the walls of this new space. Video cameras hung from the stone ceilings in all four corners, each pointed to the center.

Panic banged in her chest.

Whatever happens here is interesting enough for him to record it.

Exhausted by her struggle, her mouth and throat dry from the rag, she took a moment to calm her breathing. She took two deep breaths through her nose, closing her eyes to imagine she *wasn't* bound and gagged on the floor of an underground boxing ring.

Catriona found it difficult to fantasize about a better situation with the zip-ties eating into the flesh around her wrists and her jaw aching from the pressure of the rag stuffed in her mouth.

What were those mental tricks people used to shift their thoughts from bad situations?

She could imagine she was bound and gagged on a tropical beach...

Think. I need a plan. At some point, he's going to cut these zip-ties and—

Catriona felt the mat beside her dip and opened her eyes. Volkov stood beside her with a roll of tape in his hands. She lay on her back as he bent at the waist and peered into her face, his cheeks coloring.

He held the tape out for her to see. "Do you want me to wrap your hands?"

He jerked the cloth from her mouth and she gasped for air.

"Do you want me to wrap your hands?" he repeated.

"I don't understand," she croaked, the words sticking in her throat. She chewed at her tongue to make more spit.

"You're a fighter, yes? So we fight. You are very strong girl. I can tell. What you did to Peter." He laughed with what sounded like genuine mirth. He poked her on the nose. "You'll be the best one yet. A real challenge."

Catriona jerked her face away from him. "You want to *box* me?"

"Kickbox, right? I can fight in many styles. I want you to fight in the style that suits you. That's why I ask about your hands. I want you to be comfortable. The way you usually fight. I want this to be fair."

"*Fair.*" Catriona repeated the word, baffled that Volkov thought fighting a girl a fraction of his size, who hadn't eaten since the night before, in an unfamiliar underground gym, was *fair*.

She rolled on her side to better see him without straining her neck. "Why?"

"Why do I want it to be fair?" He pulled a pocketknife from the waistband of his shorts and cut the ties from around her ankles. Tilting her to a sitting position, he cut the ties around her wrists.

Catriona rubbed at her wrists as Volkov took a step back, placing himself between her and the ladder. She guessed that meant the other two archways only led deeper into his lair, not to additional exits.

He smiled down at her as if she were a work of art he'd finished. Removing his silky red robe, he allowed it to slip to the ground and land beside her feet, revealing a muscular physique dotted with black tattoos.

Catriona looked away, unwilling to give him the satisfaction of her attention. She rose to her feet, wobbling on the matt as she struggled to find her balance. "If I win, you'll let Mo and me go?"

Volkov barked with laughter. "If you win it means I'm *dead*, so you can do whatever you like. See there?" Volkov pointed to one of the archways. "My pistol is in there. If you knock me unconscious, you take the gun. Kill me and any men in the house. Take Mo and go home."

"And if I lose?"

He shrugged. "If you lose, Mo will return to her husband as soon as he provides me with the network for the clothing."

"And me?"

He smiled. "You'll see."

Volkov rubbed once at his crotch as if something had stirred there.

Catriona's limbs tingled a second time. Electricity, provided by fear.

A silence fell as Catriona's gaze swept over the room, searching for any advantage.

Walls. Mats. Video cameras. Lights on the ceiling. A classic brass boxing ring bell gong mounted to the wall. Archways to other places I don't want to go.

Behind Volkov stood the ladder to freedom. She needed to move him away from it.

She licked her lips. "Do you have any food? I haven't eaten in over a day. I don't think that makes for a fair fight."

Volkov frowned. "Peter did not feed you?"

"I didn't eat the sandwich. I was afraid it was poisoned."

Volkov nodded. "Smart girl. I have poisoned the food before. Though this time, no." He held up a finger. "I have an energy bar in the other room."

He walked to one of the opposite archways, glancing back at her often.

"Stay there."

Catriona offered a slight nod of her head.

Sure. I'll stay right here and wait for you to beat me unconscious.

As he ducked through the arch, she bolted for the hatch.

Hope proved short-lived.

The moment her fingers found the ladder, Volkov slammed into her from behind, pressing her body painfully against the rungs. She cried out as he pulled back her arms, using his weight to pin her. The zip-ties tightened around her wrists once more.

She felt his lips brush her ear. "I knew you would run. I'm so glad you did."

"Help!" Catriona screamed toward the hatch hovering feet above her head. She bobbed her head, trying to rid her neck of his hot breath.

Volkov leaned back, wrapping one hand across her mouth and another around her waist. She tried to bite him, kicking at his shins with her heels as he dragged her back into the larger room. He threw her to the mat.

"Scream all you like. No one can hear through the stone."

Catriona fell on her shoulder, scrambling to find her feet beneath her again. She tried to stand and he kicked her back to a sitting position. When she tried again he stepped on her leg and she cried out.

Volkov dangled a wrapped energy bar above her.

"Wrapped. Untampered."

He removed his foot from her leg.

Catriona sat, breathing heavily. She tried to flip the hair from her face as he opened the energy bar and broke off a piece.

Stepping to the side to avoid potential kicks from her unbound legs, he squatted down and put a hand on the back of her head, pushing the bar into her mouth.

She spat it out.

He snatched the food from the mat and pushed down on her chin with the butt of his palm. The pressure proved more than she could bear. She opened her mouth, terrified he'd unhinge her jaw. He shoved in the chunk of the energy bar, closed her jaw, and covered her lips with his palm.

She heard him whisper behind her. "Swallow it."

He pressed his thumb into the tender spot at the base of her skull until she chewed the bar and swallowed.

He moved in front of her, victorious.

She stared at him from beneath a lowered brow, her jaw aching. "You think it's a fair fight because you force-fed me half an energy bar?"

He held up the other half of the bar. "Are you going to finish the rest the easy way or the hard way?"

He held the bar to her lips. She could feel her body shaking with anger and humiliation.

Might as well get what energy I can from this.

She bit off another piece and chewed. When she was done, he popped the last piece into her mouth.

He walked away from her, brushing the granola from his hands. "I'll give you a moment to compose yourself."

She curled her legs beneath her. "If you want to be beaten by a woman, why not just ask me?"

He chuckled. "It isn't that." He leaned back on his heels, rocking, his hands behind his back. "I tried putting the woman in power. I tried a dom...domin...what is the word? The women with the whips?"

"Dominatrix?"

"Yes. I didn't like it at all."

"So it's *hurting* women that turns you on."

He smiled. "Da. But I like a *challenge*."

In his words, Catriona spotted a glimmer of hope. "What if I refused to fight?"

He shook his head. "I said I don't like an unfair fight, but I get bored and make do if I have to."

Catriona took a deep breath and expelled it. Her attention drifted to the roll of tape he'd presented to her earlier, now laying a few feet away on the mat.

She looked at Volkov.

"I'd like my hands taped."

CHAPTER TWENTY-FOUR

Catriona held out her hands as Volkov wrapped them in flex tape. He was good at it.

He must wrap hands as often as he zip-ties.

She wasn't sure she wanted to explore any more of his unusual skill sets.

He had to be a fighter. The mats, the professional-looking bell, the tape, his sinewy body—the man had spent some time in gyms.

She couldn't let their battle begin on even ground. She'd have to find a way to take him by surprise. Now wasn't the time. He'd untied her hands so he could wrap them, but he'd zipped her ankles to make up for it.

It didn't hurt to get her hands taped. Maybe she could avoid a few broken knuckles. Maybe it would relax him—allowing him to run through a ritual with her. Maybe even soften him to her, if that was possible.

Most importantly, the taping of her hands gave her time to *think*.

Sean had said he, she, and Kilty somehow inspired people to be their best.

At the moment, she couldn't help but feel her little superpower had left her.

She looked up at the cameras in the corners of the room.

He records everything.

If she could watch one of the recordings, maybe she could gain insight into his ritual or fighting style.

He finished her right hand and she flexed it, checking the tightness. It felt perfect.

"Do you keep the recordings here?" she asked as he tapped

her left hand, asking her to raise it.

Volkov's brow scrunched. "What do you mean?"

She nodded to the cameras. "The other girls." She chose her next words carefully. "Can I watch?"

Volkov appeared surprised.

And, *something else.*

Flattered?

Perhaps.

Pleased.

The corner of his mouth curled. "You want to see the other girls?"

She nodded.

"Why?"

Because I want to know how to beat you.

She did her best to look titillated at the prospect of watching his amateur films.

"I want to see you in action," she said, her voice falling to a whisper. She hoped it sounded seductive. In truth, her voice had simply failed her, the depth of the lie nearly too far to reach her lips.

Volkov finished wrapping the tape on her right knuckles and stood. He held out his hand. "Come with me."

She allowed him to pull her to her feet.

"Put out your hands."

She hesitated. She hated permitting herself to be bound again but watching his videos could be her best shot at beating him.

She held out her hands. Volkov slipped another zip tie from the pocket of his robe and locked her wrists.

Slipping a hand behind her knees, he lifted her, carrying her through the archway into a new room, roughly ten-by-ten feet. The floor and walls had no padding. He set her down in a large leather chair positioned in front of a television. Against the far wall, a laptop sat on a small desk. Long orange extension cords led from a power strip up through a hole in the ceiling.

A small fishbowl sat tucked on the lower shelf of a wooden plant stand beside the television. Volkov bent down to hook a finger in it before holding it out to her.

He shook it. Inside, six or seven thumb drives rattled. "Pick one."

These are the recordings?

"Da."

The drives were all black but for one red. She wasn't sure if it mattered which she picked. She wanted to watch the one that exposed the most about his fighting style and tricks if there were any.

Chances were good the better he thought he fought, the more he'd favor that movie.

"Do you have a favorite?" she asked.

He shrugged.

She hoped his apathy meant all the clips were similar. If his beatings were ritualistic, maybe she could find a pattern. Anticipating his moves could be the difference between escaping, or dying at the hands of a sick freak in an underground cave.

She looked out into the fighting chamber.

No one will ever find me.

She suspected each drive held the final moments of a young woman's life. It was possible Volkov's victims were all out there somewhere, alive, too traumatized or frightened to go to the police.

Probably not.

Volkov had to know the odds of remaining a free man sank each time he sent a girl home.

Catriona forced another playful smile and reached in to grab one of the black thumb drives, reasoning if the red was an anomaly, it would be less useful to her research. She handed the drive to him and he smiled, rolling it through his fingers before plugging it into the back of the television.

She watched him. He appeared pleased with himself. Relaxed. On a small table next to her chair sat a remote control. Volkov snatched it and hit play.

Catriona pulled her eyes from him and pointed her attention at the screen.

She recognized the room. The clip had been edited to include angles from each of the four cameras she'd seen mounted in the corners.

An Asian woman stood in the center of the mat. Catriona guessed her to be in her early twenties. Her tight-fitting, braless spandex top and leopard tube skirt said *hooker*. Maybe *stripper*. Maybe a girl on her way to the club. It was hard to tell these days.

Eyes red and swollen from crying, she sobbed, staring at the boxing gloves on her hands. The next shot showed Volkov looking very much like he did now, wearing only wrestling shorts. His body appeared oiled, his skin glistening beneath the lights.

He'll be hard to grapple with if he's covered in baby oil.

She noticed he wore no gloves.

"Aren't you going to put gloves on?" asked the girl, as if reading Catriona's mind.

"I choose not to," he said.

The angle switched to a camera pointed at Volkov's face, though there was no cameraman to zoom in on him.

He knows right where to stand for his close-up.

On the screen, the corners of Volkov's mouth pointed down. The playful attitude she'd experienced was nowhere to be seen.

This Volkov meant business.

Great. My power to encourage the best in people only inspired him to whistle while he kills me.

The girl's eyebrows raised. "Is that right? I mean I thought whatever I chose you had to—"

"I never said that," said Volkov off-camera.

Volkov glanced at Catriona and she did her best not to react.

There it was, hint number one.

Don't choose the gloves.

Most people, when handed gloves and told they were about to fight, would put *on* the gloves. There was no way for them to know Volkov had no intention of padding *his* blows.

Volkov's attention returned to the screen. He must have seen the movie a thousand times, but his expression was as eager as that of a child about to watch his first summer blockbuster.

On the screen, Volkov walked to the bell on the wall and, following a dramatic pause, rang it.

The girl melted to her knees. "I don't understand. I don't want to do this."

Catriona could barely make out the words through her sobs.

Volkov approached her.

"Please. Fight," he coaxed her.

"I don't—"

He slapped the girl so suddenly and with such force, Catriona sucked in a breath. Volkov looked at her, eager to see her horror. She dropped the hand she'd raised to cover her mouth, angry at herself for giving him what he so clearly wanted.

He paused the movie. "You don't approve?"

She shrugged and motioned to the screen as if she were dismissing an unproductive employee. "I'm disgusted she didn't fight back."

He smiled. "Da. *You* understand. I knew you would."

Volkov moved to Catriona and put his hand on her head, stroking her hair once before hitting play again. Catriona's mouth went dry.

The movie continued that way; the girl crying, Volkov slapping her to the ground and demanding she rise. At one point she weakly pounded her fists on his chest, which he allowed her to do, his head back as if he were basking in the sun. When her arms grew tired and she stopped, he punched her in the face. She spun like a top and fell to her knees, ending on her back. She didn't move.

On the screen, Volkov straightened her legs and laid her arms to her side, posing her on the ground. He stood over her, hands in the air, nodding to an audience not there. He made a muscle with his right arm, his fist hovering near his temple. He lined himself up with the girl on the ground and fell on her, leading with his elbow, smashing into her mouth.

The girl awoke with a start, screaming, flipping to her side. Catriona saw her spit teeth on the mat.

It took every ounce of strength to keep herself from covering her mouth in horror.

The interaction between the two people on the screen grew darker. Volkov tore away the young woman's clothes. After that, Catriona pretended to watch, but averted her eyes, humming a song in her head to drown out the girl's shrieks of pain.

When the screaming stopped, she turned to Volkov.

"One more?" she begged. Her chest felt tight with nerves and nausea. She worried he could see through her frozen smile.

He did not.

Instead, he grinned and held out the fishbowl. "One more."

The chance to watch his previous victories with his future victim was too good for Volkov to deny himself. After all, these weren't the sort of movies you could invite *anyone* to watch.

If he sensed her fascination with his videos was a lie, he

chose not to admit it to himself.

Catriona picked the red drive this time.

Volkov popped it into the back of the television and she watched a very similar story unfold. This girl also appeared to be a lady of the night. It made sense, of course, as fewer people would ask questions about missing hookers. This young woman was larger, possibly of mixed race. She fought hard, but still, Volkov outweighed her by a good seventy pounds. When he decided to attack, it wasn't long before she lay on the ground, groaning, unable to rise.

He ended the fighting portion of his ritual with the same elbow drop. As soon as he posed over the girl, preparing to fall, Catriona averted her eyes.

Her skin crawled. Anxiety dreams of losing teeth were not unfamiliar to her, and the idea that it could happen for real—

"Again?" she asked, hoping to push her fate at his hands farther into the future.

Volkov moved between her and the television to place a hand on each of her cheeks. She felt the muscles in her face twitch with revulsion.

He spoke in the low, soft tone of a lover. "No. I don't think I can wait any longer."

Volkov removed the drive from the television and dropped it back into the bowl.

Catriona motioned to the screen. "What happened to them?"

Volkov opened a drawer in the desk and pulled out a bottle of baby lotion. He poured some into his palm and began to rub it on his arms and chest.

His tattoos were easier to see now: Eight-pointed stars at the tips of his clavicle, an enormous church spanning from belly to chest, coffins lining the front of the church. Over one kidney, a woman stood holding a fishing line, the hook grabbing the back of her dress to expose her legs. Two mermaids frolicked over his left hip.

He smiled, staring at her as he slathered his abdomen with the oil. "You'll see."

CHAPTER TWENTY-FIVE

"What are you doing here?"

Fiona placed her keys on the marble kitchen island of her apartment, scowling at Rune. He stood, hands in his pockets, staring through the glass wall overlooking Parasol Pictures.

At least, she assumed his eyes were open. Her father wasn't the most predictable person in the world.

Rune spoke without turning. "One down."

What? She was in no mood for his nonsense.

"How did you get into my apartment?" she asked.

No response.

Fiona's teeth clenched. She'd been hoping her father would find her, hoping *together* they could accomplish quite a bit. But now that he'd arrived, acting as if he *owned* her, any chance of warm and fuzzy father-daughter moments were fading fast.

Rune turned, the power of his pale eyes dimmed by his backlit form. Fiona could barely see his shadowed facial features, which she appreciated.

She didn't like his eyes. She didn't remember them being so *icy.*

"Sean is gone," Rune said, scratching at the neck of his ridiculous high-buttoned flannel shirt.

"Gone? Gone where?"

He shrugged. "Where is the Highlander?"

"Where—?"

Before she could finish her sentence, Rune began to unbutton his shirt. He pulled it off, exposing his bird-breasted frame. To Fiona, he looked like one of the creatures scientists sometimes found on the bottom of the ocean floor. Boney, pale, nearly translucent.

She didn't remember her mother very well, but she thought she recalled her being a beauty.

How she produced me and Catriona with this cave frog as the sperm donor—

"I'm hot. I need a shirt. Get me one I can wear." Rune threw his flannel to the ground and rubbed at his throat.

Fiona's anger skipped to a new level. She opened her mouth to tell him she was *done* being talked to in such a demeaning manner, but all she did was gape.

Her father's neck was covered in *smiles.*

Some thin, some thick, one overlapping the next, scars of varying darkness, each one running across his neck, the ends curling up as they disappeared behind his throat.

Fiona raised her hand to point. "What is *that*?"

Rune looked up to find her pointing. His hands once again raised to his throat.

"It's necessary."

"What's necessary? Who did that to you?"

Rune held her in his steady gaze. "I did."

"Why?"

"You know why."

She scoffed, tired of the mysteries surrounding the man. "The hell I do, you *freak*—"

Rune's expression twisted into a tight knot. He took a step forward, a threatening advance that stopped Fiona cold.

He thrust his head forward, squinting at her as if she had morphed into a creature he didn't recognize. "Have you learned nothing while I've been gone?"

Fiona opened her purse, looking for nothing, her nervous fingers desperate to find something to do. "What was it I was supposed to learn?"

"To travel we have to *die. Nearly* die."

"Nearly—" Fiona paused, her hand still hanging in her purse. The source of Rune's smiles flashed in her mind's eye, swinging against a stark white background.

Nooses.

Rune hung himself to trigger time travel.

What kind of sicko...?

He was the man on whom she'd hung her hopes? The man she thought was destined to provide her with direction? Give her a sense of purpose?

"Why would you do that to yourself? Why are you making

yourself jump—"

"Because I need to learn. I need to grow. I have to become complete—"

"Why?"

"*So I can kill them all.*" Rune swung his arm wide, sending her favorite lamp crashing to the ground.

Fiona gasped, her hands rising to cover her mouth.

"Oh, I loved that lamp." She took a step forward to gather the pieces on the ground, stopping as she felt Rune's pale eyes locked on her. Something about his look said *she* might be lumped in with *them all.*

The people he wanted to kill.

Fiona straightened and rocked her weight back against the raised breakfast bar counter.

She cleared her throat. "Who do you want to kill?"

Rune's shoulders squared. "Everyone not strong enough to resist me. The weaklings."

"What does that even mean?"

"Survival of the fittest."

Fiona nodded, pretending to understand.

He's insane. How did I forget that? How did I forget why I ran away from him in the first place?

She held out her hands, patting the air down with her palms in an attempt to calm her father.

"Just so you know, I'm not in for this."

"*In for this?*"

"I'm out. I thought we could work together but it sounds like you have a plan I'm not prepared—"

"What?"

She took a measured breath.

"We have different *goals.* We're not on the same page. I don't want to kill everyone. I don't care about *everyone.* I just want my share of the fame and fortune. My career—"

Rune took half a step forward, his hands curling into fists. "Your *career?*"

Fiona felt a chill run down the back of her neck.

You can do this. You've left him before.

"My career is—"

Rune took two long strides toward her, too fast for her to stop him. He moved, *wrong.* Like a stop-action cartoon played at high speed. He was on her before her mind could process his movement.

Bony fingers wrapped around her neck. They felt too long. She could feel them overlapping above her nape. Fiona grabbed his wrists, peeling at his grip, her gasps for air hindered by the pressure of his thumbs on her windpipe.

Rune leaned forward, bending her back against the countertop. Her spine felt as though it might snap. Lowering his face close to hers, he hissed, his face red with strain.

"Let it happen. Think of a place nearby. *Want* that place and that's where you'll go. *Want it.*"

Fiona's left hand shot to the side, reaching until her fingers found her purse. She pushed her hand inside the bag, feeling for something, *anything* she could use.

Her touch slid along something smooth and hard.

My autograph pen.

Not long after she'd booked her first television show, a little girl had asked her for her signature. She'd been giddy at the prospect of signing her name, but she didn't carry a pen at the time, and she'd sworn to never miss the opportunity again. She bought herself the most perfect, black, Monte Blanc pen she could find, carrying it always.

Hooking the pen into her palm, she worked the cap off to reveal the point.

He squeezed. Her vision grew dark. Starbursts popped against murky black.

Her arm jerked from the purse.

She stabbed.

The pen embedded into the side of Rune's throat, plunging through layers of rough scar tissue.

Her father roared and released his grip on her. First, the right hand, which slapped his neck as he stumbled back. Then the left.

Fiona ducked beneath that left hand and ran for the door. Behind her, she heard Rune wailing with anger.

He's coming.

She fiddled with the doorknob for what felt like forever. Finally, her palms found purchase and she turned the oval globe, flinging the door behind her as she ran into the hall.

She glanced at the large, silver elevator doors, remembering every time she'd ever pushed the recall button. Calculating the time it took to arrive.

No time.

Running to the stairs, she pushed open the door. She heard

Rune behind her.

"Fiona!"

She slipped, nearly falling on her rear as she hit the first set of stairs. Catching herself on the railing, she kicked off her heels and ran down the remaining flights. She couldn't hear anyone behind her now. She didn't know if he'd taken the elevator.

On the ground floor, she pushed open the door and burst into the lobby.

"Did my father come out of the elevator?" she asked as she ran by the deskman.

"What? Miss Fiona, no, what...?"

She didn't stop. She ran through another door to the garage and jumped into her car, thrilled her secure, private parking had inspired the habit of leaving her keys in the coffee mug holder cup.

One of the little luxuries of being rich—you didn't worry people might rummage through your car at night.

She started the Lexus and pulled from her spot, tires squealing on the smooth pavement.

The exit's iron gate bars lifted as she rolled toward them and she slid beneath them, turning into the guest parking lot leading to the front of the building.

There he is.

Rune stumbled through the front door like a zombie, his hand still on his neck, his naked chest covered in blood.

Fiona screamed and jerked her wheel to the left to avoid him. It wasn't kindness that made her swerve. She felt sure if she hit him, somehow he would only be *more mad.*

Passing him, she looked in her rearview mirror in time to see him fall to his knees.

She didn't feel herself crossing the threshold from the parking lot into the street. That little bump she'd experienced a hundred times before. All she felt was a car plowing into the front passenger side of her Lexus, sending her spinning.

When her car stopped rotating she didn't take a moment to find her bearings. Instead, she clawed at the door like an animal, until her fingers hooked on the handle and she spilled into the street. Her knees ached as they hit the pavement.

A moment later she was back on her feet.

"Are you okay?"

A man in a baseball cap stood outside the car that had hit her. She didn't know the brand of his vehicle. Didn't recognize the logo. *Something cheap.* A child stared at her through the window of the back seat.

Fiona stood a moment, unsure which way to go. Down the block, she spotted the ornate entrance to Parasol Pictures.

Security. Safety.

Fiona bolted down the street, barefoot, as fast as she could run.

CHAPTER TWENTY-SIX

"I guess I don't need to ask you if you want the gloves," said Volkov, chuckling. He traded his bottle of oil for a small wooden box, pulled from his desk drawer. Opening it, he retrieved what looked like a ball of white powder in plastic wrap. Shaking some of the powder into his palm, he snorted it before rewrapping the ball and placing it back in the box.

Catriona felt as if she'd fallen into shock.

None of this can be real.

She couldn't be watching a man lather himself with oil and snort drugs as he prepares to—

Those movies.

She looked away and tried to make her mind go blank. When she looked back, he was staring at her, awaiting an answer about the gloves.

"No."

Catriona watched him slide the box back into the desk drawer.

"What did you think about the end of the videos?" he asked, finishing the sentence with a sniff as he pinched his nose.

She found she couldn't answer. Her ability to *pretend* had left her. She refused to look at him.

He let his question die.

"Ready?"

Volkov flipped a switch mounted to the wall and the lights in the center fighting room blasted into a new gear. He liked his victims to be well lit for the camera.

He lifted her from the chair.

"No. No, no no—" The words spilled from Catriona's lips. When she began to struggle, he pushed his nails into her skin and gripped, crushing her against him until she could barely breathe.

He walked her into the large room and dropped her in the center.

"Stay there."

Bound hand and foot, she didn't have much choice. He pulled a tiny pocket knife from the band of his shorts and cut the tie around her feet.

He took a step back, pulling her hands out with him as he went. When he was standing just out of reach, he put the knife behind the tie and pulled the blade through the plastic.

Catriona's hands dropped to her sides and she took a step back.

They stood facing each other. Catriona rubbed her wrists. Her limbs felt numb, but she knew it was fear and not the zip-ties that had left them tingling.

She stood, heart in her throat, mentally replaying the videos of the girls who'd come before her, hoping her ability to recall things in detail would allow her to spot a misstep in his attack. *Something* that would give her the advantage.

Catriona now knew Volkov fought in a traditional boxing style. He rarely used his feet to kick, though he'd had some experience wrestling, judging by the holds in which he'd wrapped the second woman during their fierce battle.

Catriona hoped her kickboxing style might prove an advantage. If the color-coding of the thumb drives meant anything—if red was reserved for women who fought back—then he wasn't used to a challenge. Volkov could brag that he loved a good fight, but he preyed on hookers—women who were often tired, malnourished, and suffering the effects of drugs and alcohol use.

Coward.

Volkov stood before her, bouncing one pec and then the other before repeating. His eyes danced in his skull. His countenance was *joyful.*

Catriona took a deep breath.

Concentrate. You can do this.

This man brutalized women. He ordered Broch's death—

Catriona realized an awful truth. If she died in this sick fight club pit, Sean would never know what happened to *either* of them.

He'd be devastated.

She could only hope if something did happen, Sean would find his way to Volkov and destroy him.

It wouldn't do *her* much good, but it was a nice thought.

No.

Wrong thinking.

Don't imagine Sean coming after Volkov.

I am going to destroy him.

Volkov took a step back and grabbed a small hammer hanging from the bell mounted on the wall. He hit the bell, once. She recognized the sound from the beginning of the videos she'd watched.

It had started.

Volkov raised his fists and circled them in front of his nose like an old-timey Marquess of Queensbury rules boxer. He looked cartoonish.

He's toying with me.

Already he wasn't following his pattern. He'd been very serious with the other women.

Would all his tricks be new today?

Volkov motioned for her to come forward.

"Do it. Come at me."

Catriona held up her hands and circled with him. She preferred to let him make the first move.

Really, she preferred to circle endlessly and never have to fight the psychopath at all.

Volkov rushed her and she kicked, instinctively, catching him on his hip. He laughed and returned to his stance.

He stepped in again and tried to slap her face, again, toying with her. She blocked him easily and moved away.

Moving forward, he tried boxing her into the corner of the room. She sensed the trap, ducked, and moved away.

Volkov bounced on his toes.

"You can't avoid me forever."

He rushed forward before the end of his sentence, swinging wildly, left and right. She blocked one, partially blocked the second, and took a glancing blow to her cheekbone as she kicked him in the stomach, just missing his groin.

He rolled back and made a tsking noise, shaking his finger at her. "Naughty girl. Not below the belt."

Good luck with that.

She reasoned it would be hard for him to rape her battered body if she kicked his dick off first.

Lunging forward, Volkov tried to wrap his arms around her. She made him pay for his playfulness and connected with an uppercut and, turning, threw an elbow into his solar plexus. He coughed, doubling over and clutching his stomach, trying to pull back. She grabbed a handful of his hair and tried to ram his face into her knee. He twisted so the blow glanced off the side of his head and backhanded her as he spun away. Catriona's head snapped with the blow and she tasted bitter iron in her mouth.

She turned to refocus and found him behind her, hand raised to strike. With nowhere to circle, she scurried through the only doorway left unexplored. As she stumbled into the room the lights turned on, triggered by a motion sensor. Her foot knocked into something unstable and she twisted, searching for solid ground.

Catriona fell to her knees, finding herself hovering precariously over a pit in the floor of the chamber, now half-covered with a piece of plywood. A horrific stench rose from the uncovered portion. Catriona gagged and covered her mouth and nose with her hand.

Lights above her head beamed down into the pit as she peered over the edge.

Six feet below, the blotchy face of a girl stared up at her, the eyes white and glazed, neon-yellow eyeshadow still smeared beneath her eyebrows. A still, pale hand jut from the murky depths beside her, standing like a white rose in a murky field of black.

An oubliette. That's where he threw the girls' bodies. There they lay, heaped together, cursed to spend eternity in his dungeon after the horror and humiliation of their deaths.

"Get out of there. It isn't your time...*yet*," teased Volkov from the fighting room.

She looked around the space. There was nowhere to run. The hole in the floor was the only additional area, and *down* wasn't an option.

She moved to the edge of the doorway.

"Step back so I can come out."

"I have. I'm in the center of the room. See?"

She poked out her head and saw him standing, in the center of the room as promised, bouncing on his toes, waiting.

"Were they dead when they went in there?" she asked. The words sounded pathetic leaving her lips. She hadn't been able to stop herself from asking.

He shrugged. "Mostly."

"Most? Or *Mostly*?"

"Both."

She stepped out and he motioned to her.

"Take your spot. We begin again."

CHAPTER TWENTY-SEVEN

Dez put her hand on Broch's arm.

"There's something else I should probably tell you about Volkov."

They'd been sitting in Dez's car, parked down the block from Volkov's safe house, for half an hour, watching. The situation seemed calm there. A man sat on the porch, smoking one cigarette after the other. Inside, another man moved by the window from time to time. There was no sign of Volkov. No sign that Catriona and Mo might be inside.

Broch was frustrated and full of nervous energy, his knee still finding room to bounce in the cramped space of Dez's car. He didn't want to wait. Dez had begged him for a half-hour of surveillance before they went charging in.

His mind was elsewhere when she touched him.

"Whit?"

Something about the expression on Dez's face made his chest tighten with fear for Catriona.

Dez took a deep breath and exhaled. "I wasn't going to tell you because, well, because I figured you wouldn't want to hear, but it hit me if we go in there—"

"Juist tell me whit it is."

She nodded. "Right. Sorry."

Another deep breath, and she began. "Volkov is a loner. The Russian mob doesn't want anything to do with him because...I don't know. He's messed up in the head."

"How?"

"I don't know the details. But I do know one thing about him. He likes to hurt women."

Broch swallowed. "Ah've prepared myself that Catriona

micht be hurt."

"I don't mean just *hurt*. Women go missing around him. Permanently. A lot."

"Howfur dae ye ken this?"

"How do I ken it?"

"*Know.*"

"Oh." Dez sniffed. "I had a friend who went missing after going with him. She was a stripper. No one realized she was gone for a couple of days. Then I heard she was in the hospital. She didn't make it."

"Volkov murdered her?"

"More than killed her. I went to see her. Her injuries..." Dez shook her head as if she wanted to break loose the memory and fling it away. "After, I asked around and heard Volkov was famous for this sort of thing. He's a legend around the strip clubs. Sort of a boogeyman."

Broch didn't know what a boogeyman was, but it didn't sound good. He looked at the house. The glow of the porch man's cigarette bobbed in the darkness.

"We need tae gae in."

"I'd like to watch more. It doesn't look like Volkov's in there."

"Bit whit if he is?"

The thought that Catriona might be inside, suffering, while he sat outside—

Broch put his hand on the door handle. "We need tae gae."

"Okay. Wait. We need a plan. They're going to spot you a mile away. You and your skirt."

"It's nae a skirt."

"Whatever."

"And they willnae see me."

"Fine. But let's be smart. The guy on the porch won't know me. You go around the houses and come over the side of the porch behind him. I'll distract him."

Broch nodded. Any plan that got him out of the car and closer to Catriona worked for him. He had his door open before Dez could finish her sentence.

Crossing the street, he cut between two residences several lots down from Volkov's safe house. The first house didn't have a fence in the backyard, so he ran through, skirting a plastic child's pool and a littering of toys. A chain-link fence encircled the next lot. He jumped it. As he jogged through the yard, he spotted a little girl staring at him through the back door screen. He waved and she smiled, waving back. He climbed over the fence on the opposite side to find himself next to Volkov's property.

The six-foot wooden fence surrounding Volkov's backyard was too flimsy to jump and too solid to break through. Broch stood on his toes and peered over it. The yard was empty. He could see a large screened-in porch, the glow from the rooms inside the house illuminating a smattering of patio furniture.

He crept to the end of the fence and entered Volkov's sideyard.

He reached the front porch and crouched down, peering between the thick cement railing that edged it. The guard no longer sat in his chair. He'd moved to the top of the stairs. Broch could hear Dez talking to him, laughing the way women did when flirting.

Broch grabbed the top of the porch railing and lifted himself until he could swing a leg over the edge. Lowering himself onto the porch, he crept toward the man flirting with Dez. As he neared his prey, Broch saw Dez's eyes flick in his direction. She tried to play it off, but the damage had been done.

The man turned.

Sae much fae the element of surprise.

Broch snapped his palm into the air, breaking the man's nose and then covering his mouth as he tried to yell. Broch pulled his head into the crook of his arm, choking him as he dragged him deeper onto the porch. He held him there, his back against the house, bobbing his head left and right to avoid the man's flailing hands until his foe went limp.

Dez looked up and down the street and then moved onto the porch.

"Did you kill him?" she whispered.

Broch huffed. "Nae. Ah wid hae, bit Catriona said ah shouldn't murdurr fowk if ah kin hulp it."

Dez scowled. "She had to *tell* you that?" She glanced at the man. "And she probably didn't mean the guys holding her hostage."

Crouching beneath the large front window, Dez peered inside.

"I see one dude on a sofa. The one we've been watching. I think he's asleep. No sign of Volkov."

Broch tried the door and found it open.

Pulling a gun from her waistband, Dez moved to him. "On three. One—"

Broch opened the creaky door and the man on the sofa turned his head toward him.

"Who are you?" he asked.

As the man scrambled to his feet, wobbly from sleeping, Broch stepped forward and punched him hard in the face. The guard fell, tucked between the sofa and the table where he'd been resting his feet.

"Shhh," hissed Dez. She had her gun raised as she poked her head into the other rooms.

"Kitchen's clear," she whispered to him as she moved to the next doorway.

Broch leaned over and grabbed the guard by his shirt, lifting him to peer into his face. The man's head lolled as if it were attached by a noodle, potato chip crumbs stuck to his cheek.

He's nae goan anywhur.

Broch dropped him with a thud to the ground.

Dez slipped down a short hall to the right and reappeared a moment later.

"Clear."

She glanced at a table beside Broch and pointed to it. "Look."

He glanced at a pile of plastic strips sitting next to the ugliest lamp he'd ever seen. He looked back at Dez. "Whit?"

She rolled her eyes. "They're zip-ties. Tie up those two in case they wake up."

Broch's attention moved from the zip-ties to the door in the center of the archway.

It had a padlock on it.

Dez went to the left and appeared again, almost bumping into him as he approached the door.

"That room's clear. Did you tie them?"

"Na."

She huffed and followed his gaze to the padlock on the door. "Yeah, I think that's our winner. You don't mind if I make sure the house is clear first, do you?"

Broch ignored her and put his ear to the door.

"Catriona?" he called.

A panic voice rose from within. "It's Mo."

Dez stepped back and pointed her gun at the door. She

nodded to Broch. "I'm ready."

"Staun back fae the door," Broch called to Mo.

He gave Mo a moment to move before kicking. The hinge holding the lock ripped from the wood and the door flew open, bouncing off the wall behind.

Mo stood in the back corner of the small windowless room. The space was empty but for two paper plates, two plastic bottles, and Mo herself.

Mo threw her arms around him.

"Thank God you're here. These people are *animals*. We thought you were dead."

"Catriona?" he asked.

She looked up at him, grimacing. "They took her. She wasn't out there?"

"Where?"

"I don't know. I woke up and that big man was walking out the door with her."

"Volkov?"

She nodded. "That's his name. The one from the warehouse."

Broch scowled at Dez. "He wis here all along."

She frowned. "Sorry."

Broch spotted a smear of blood on the wall and felt his pulse quicken. He looked at Mo and she shook her head.

"Not hers. She beat up one of the guys. She wasn't hurt the last time I saw her but the man who took her..." Mo fell silent. "It was only about an hour ago."

Broch walked back into the living room. "We didnae see them leave," he muttered, searching the house for doors they might have missed.

Mo followed him into the living room and spotted Dez. "Dez, Alain sent you?"

Dez grunted. "Something like that."

Broch strode into the kitchen and eyed the rows of lower cabinets, dreading the idea of opening them in search of Catriona.

Thay couldn't hae gaen far.

The pantry door was missing and the shelving left no room for anyone to hide.

Broch pushed open the back door and entered the screened porch he'd noticed while peering over the fence. He left through a screen door and visually traced the edge of the yard's perimeter. The fencing was visible by the light in the kitchen. There didn't seem to be anywhere to hide in the dirt-filled backyard.

Broch turned to re-enter the house, pausing when something about the angle of the wicker sofa on the porch struck him as odd. He noticed drag marks on the floor where the sofa had been moved.

Pushing it further away, he spotted the outline of a square on the floor.

A trap door.

He dropped to his knees and pressed his ear against the floor, his fingers scrambling along the wood, searching for a way to open the hatch.

"Dez!" he called to the other room.

Dez appeared from the kitchen.

"Yeah?"

"Tak' Mo tae the car. Git her oot o' 'ere."

"What are you doing?"

"Ah'm keeking fae Catriona."

As if on cue, Mo appeared behind Dez. "Let's go. I've got to get out of here."

Dez sighed and looked at Broch. "I'll take her. I'll be right back. Don't do anything stupid."

Broch nodded.

The moment Dez left the room, he pulled his knife from its sheath. With his other hand, he felt the top of the trap door until his fingers brushed over a handle embedded in the wood. He hadn't been able to see it with the sofa blocking the light from the kitchen.

He wouldn't be waiting for Dez to get back.

CHAPTER TWENTY-EIGHT

Catriona glanced down the slanted hall leading to the ladder. Could she make it to the ladder, climb it and get out in time? Maybe, if she could incapacitate him long enough...

Volkov lunged at her again, swiping with his long arms.

She tried to dodge and use his momentum against him, but the tight quarters made it difficult to move from his reach. He grabbed her around the middle and she pounded down on his chin with her fist. He ignored the first blow and pushed her to the wall. The ragged stones ate into her back, bruising her spine. She cried out, the sound of her pain acting like gasoline on the fire of Volkov's malicious intent. Laughing, he lifted her from the ground, but she twisted in the air to interrupt his body slam. He lost his balance, falling to the side to catch himself on one knee and she fell to the ground beside him.

Catriona scrambled away, trying to put enough distance between them so that she could find her feet, but Volkov was on her in an instant. He grabbed her from behind and she kicked, catching him in the chest once before he enveloped her and fell with his weight pinning her torso to the mat.

He punched her hard in the back of her head.

The world flashed white.

No no no...I can't lose consciousness.

She'd seen what happened to the unconscious girls, *twice.* He would stand over her, victorious, before falling, elbow first, cracking her teeth like fine china. Then the things she couldn't watch would happen, and she'd end up rotting in the oubliette, where no one would ever find her. If they did, by then, she'd be nothing more than a few drops of DNA on a crime scientist's slide.

The elbow drop.

That was *it.*

The move was predictable.

Catriona went limp. She hoped it wasn't too late, that he hadn't seen her move after the blow to her head.

Volkov ground his hips against her buttocks, shifting to straddle her. She could feel the tension in his thighs, knew he had his hand raised ready to hit her again. She didn't know when or where the blow would land. Staying still, defenseless, awaiting the attack, was the longest five seconds of her life.

He didn't swing.

Volkov dismounted, stepping over her with one foot to stand. She could feel the flexing of the floor pads on her right. Was he raising his hands in victory? She didn't dare look. She had to trust the pattern. He'd rolled the other girls on their backs.

Volkov kicked her in her side. She couldn't stop the rush of air escaping from her lungs but she showed no other sign of consciousness.

"Victory in the first round." Volkov clucked his tongue. "I thought you would be better."

He slid his foot under her shoulder and flipped her over, squatting to arrange her on the ground. He straightened her legs on the mat and brought her arms down at her sides.

A moment later, she felt the bounce of the mat beside her.

This is it.

His hands were raised over his head now, she was sure. She replayed the videos in her head and saw the way he bounced on his toes as he celebrated his victory.

Catriona relaxed her face muscles. She needed to risk opening her eyes. She'd never realized how hard it was to crack open an eyelid without squinting. Squinting would give her game away.

She allowed her eyelids enough slack to open naturally, feeling oddly grateful he'd punched her in the back of her head and not swollen her eyes.

Above her, Volkov turned to his imaginary audiences, represented by each wall, one by one. When his back turned to her, she lifted her chin a bit to get a better view through the thin arc of her open eye.

Volkov made his full circle and then crooked his arms like a football field goal to make muscles on either side. He glanced down at her, lining up her mouth.

He turned sideways, preparing to fall.

Catriona tried not to tense.

Like a felled tree, Volkov began to topple, his elbow screaming toward her mouth.

At the last second, Catriona rolled away and Volkov hit the empty mat. She turned and chopped hard at his throat, striking him in the Adam's apple with all her strength.

Volkov wheezed and clutched at his throat. Catriona clapped her hands together above her head to create a hammer and swung down, striking him in the testicles.

If the strike to his windpipe didn't leave him breathless, the groin shot would. She'd hit men there before. She didn't understand it, but she knew it ended fights very quickly.

Volkov jerked to a sitting position, howling, gagging, still struggling to breathe. He sounded like an amorous alley cat who'd smoked a pack of cigarettes every day through all nine lives.

Catriona twisted her body and punched him in the nose with every last trace of power in her body. He flattened to his back and she straddled him, pinning his arms to his body. Left and then right, over and over she struck at him, never giving him the chance to find his breath. He bucked, trying to throw her off of him, but she clung to him like an octopus' sucker. Her mind told her to run to the ladder, that he'd never be able to stop her in time, but enraged, for herself and the women in the oubliette, she continued to pound him, striking like a tireless machine.

"Catriona!"

The voice came from behind her. She paused for a split second, distracted from her attack. Volkov took the opportunity to whip his arm out from beneath her. His face covered in blood, he threw a blind punch, striking her in the side of the head.

The blow knocked her sideways and she struck her opposite temple on the stone wall.

The world went black.

CHAPTER TWENTY-NINE

Broch opened the trapdoor. The smell of dirt and something foul struck his nostrils.

It smelled like death.

A ladder led to the bottom of a shallow dugout. The floor appeared blue, and Broch wasn't sure what to make of that. Light shone from another source below and to the right, so he knew the cellar continued.

It has tae be a prison...

Why else would someone dig a hole like that? He'd seen no root cellars since arriving in Los Angeles. Certainly, people didn't grow and store their own food in this arid hellhole.

Every sinew in his body strained, begging for him to call out to Catriona, but he couldn't risk alarming whatever guard might be down there with her.

Volkov had to be down there.

Broch mounted the ladder and climbed into the pit. Crouching to keep from hitting his head on the ceiling, he shuffled down a ramp with the same blue padding for flooring as the first room. Something ahead of him steadily thudded.

Smack. Smack. Smack.

Poking his head into the room, he saw Catriona straddling a man, beating him with her fists.

He said the word before he could stop himself.

"Catriona!"

Catriona turned. Her mouth had begun to curl into a smile when the man beneath her struck out with his right hand, knocking her from her perch and into the wall beside them. Broch watched her head bounce off the stone.

She slumped to the ground.

Broch knew he couldn't run to her yet.

He turned his fury on the man. He knew who it was, even through the sheet of blood covering his face.

Volkov.

Volkov scrambled to his feet. The Russian wiped the blood from his eyes and roared, running at Broch like a man possessed.

Broch swung but Volkov dipped, tackling him at the waist. Hammering with his elbow, Broch struck at his attacker's shoulder. The Russian spun away from him, taking a defensive stance on the opposite side of the room. Blood dripped from a cut above his eye and Volkov slapped at it, bouncing on his toes, motioning for Broch to come forward.

"Bring it!"

Broch placed himself between Volkov and Catriona, sizing up his foe. The man was naked but for a pair of tightfitting shorts, his muscular body slick with sweat and blood and covered in tattoos. He wasn't a small man, and while his swollen face and bleeding eye implied Catriona had taken something out of him, his frenzied demeanor suggested Broch would be fighting something more than an average man.

"You ruined the best part," said Volkov licking his lips.

Broch clenched his fists. "Ah think the best part's aboot tae happen richt noo."

The two men ran at each other, grappling like bears. Broch's hands slipped on sweaty skin and Volkov punched him in the side of his jaw. Broch stumbled back against the wall, angry at himself for letting Volkov take a shot. He ran at the man again. Volkov swung and Broch blocked the blow, catching the Russian in the center of the church tattooed over his solar plexus. The air rushed out of him, but Volkov returned with a shower of furious blows. Broch did his best to block the bulk of the punches until he was able to catch the Russian with a good right. Volkov fell back, shaking his head like a wet dog, blood flying from his limp, wet hair.

Volkov spat blood on the ground. "She fought like a tiger."

Broch felt the anger rise in his blood and fought his urge to run at the man.

Be smart.

He continued to circle, planning his next attack. He didn't want to drag the fight out any longer. He needed to tend to Catriona. But he also didn't know the playing field. Didn't know what traps the dungeon might contain.

"I made her hurt. She didn't want to cry out but I made her."

Broch's patience failed him.

Nope. Ah'm gonna rush him nae.

As Broch leaped forward, Volkov flew into the air as if pulled up by a string. His body contorted as he swung his foot at Broch's head.

He fights with his feet?

Didn't matter.

Broch blocked the kick and continued forward, pinning the off-balance Russian to the wall. The kick might have taken Broch by surprise another time, but while Volkov's body continued its frenzied dance, it seemed the Russian's mind had begun to fail him. He hadn't taken into consideration the vulnerable position he'd put himself in by throwing his leg into the air against a barreling Highlander.

Broch punched his foe in the face twice before Volkov managed to block one. The Russian twisted out from beneath him, his slippery skin sliding through Broch's grasp. He scrambled away like an animal on all fours to the opposite side of the room.

Volkov whirled and put his back against the wall, appearing stunned. He wiped his face with both hands.

"You're too fast," he muttered. "Why are you so fast?"

Volkov stood near Catriona. He glanced at her.

Brock pointed at him. "Don't."

Volkov took a step toward her. Broch started forward and Volkov grabbed Catriona's hair, pulling her limp neck back, her jaw hanging slack.

Brock froze. "If ye hurt her ah'll keep ye alive until ah've broken every bone in yer body."

"I can break her neck before you take another step."

Broch swallowed. He felt confident he could put his fist through the man's skull before he could do as he threatened.

"Volkov."

The voice came from the ramp entrance.

Volkov and Broch both turned.

Dez stood there, gun pointed at the Russian.

"Do you remember Ginger?" she asked.

Volkov grinned, the gap where a tooth had been, flashing.

"I'm sorry I didn't get to finish her."

Without another word, Dez fired.

Broch saw the red dot appear on Volkov's forehead before his neck whipped back and he collapsed on Catriona.

Broch ran forward and threw the man aside, lifting Catriona's body to peer into her face.

He tapped her cheeks and brushed her blood-soaked hair from her face. "Cat. Cat, wake up."

Her eyes fluttered open.

"You're alive," she said.

He'd been thinking the same thing.

"Ah am."

"Little late getting here, though."

He smirked. "Juist in time ah think."

"Volkov?"

"Dead."

Her body relaxed in his arms.

Broch turned to Dez. "We need tae get her tae the hospital."

Dez stood over Volkov's body, her mouth hooked to the right.

"I maybe shouldn't have done that."

She kicked at the Russian's still form and glanced up at Broch.

"Felt good, though."

Catriona put a hand on Broch's cheek, grunting as he helped her sit up. She rubbed the side of her head where it had struck the wall.

"No hospital. I'm good. I'd rather go home. I just need a second. You got Mo?"

Dez nodded. "She's in the car. And I zipped up the other two." She scowled at Broch. "Since *someone* couldn't be bothered."

Broch stood and helped Catriona to her feet.

"Kin ye walk?"

She nodded and took a step. "Nothing's broken. I just feel like one big *bruise*."

Dez put her gun back into the waist of her jeans. "I need to call the cops. I need you two to stick around and back up my side of the story."

Catriona nodded. "I don't think you'll have any problems." She motioned to the archways on the opposite side of the room. "That one has thumb drives of him beating and murdering women. That one has the bodies."

Dez winced and looked at her phone. "No signal. I gotta go up." She walked up the ramp and disappeared from view.

Catriona threw herself against Broch, wrapping her arms around him and squeezing him tight.

"Urr ye a'richt?" he asked. He could feel her body shake. "Are ye crying?"

She sniffed. "It's the adrenalin."

He didn't know what to say. He wanted to pull her into his arms and carry her straight home.

He kissed her head. "My sweet bonny lass. Don't ever leave me again."

"I didn't have much choice—"

He poked a finger at her. *"Don't dae it."*

She chuckled. "Deal."

She sniffed and pulled back far enough to look up at him. "I didn't think I'd see *you* again, either."

He scoffed and cupped her cheek with his palm. "Nothin' kin tak' me away fae ye, Catriona." He smiled. "Not again."

She sucked in a sharp breath and pressed herself against him again.

"I'm sorry. I'm a little emotional right now. It's been a hell of a day."

He chuckled. "Ye stay 'ere as long as ye need."

"No." She sniffed and pulled away again. "Get me out of here."

Broch helped her up the ramp and set her at the bottom of the ladder, ready to follow her up.

He stood behind her and voiced the words playing in his head. "All ah want tae dae is grab ye 'n' haud ye."

She leaned back against him and closed her eyes.

"Thank you."

CHAPTER THIRTY

Catriona rested her head on Broch's shoulder and watched Las Vegas pass by through the window of their cab as they headed to the airport. She'd had a shower and changed, but still felt like a bruised peach left rotting under a tree. Possibly run over by a lawnmower a few times...

Welts had risen in spots she didn't remember being struck. She looked like she'd fallen off Paris's mini Eiffel tower and hit every metal rung on the way down.

"I'm sorry you didn't get to experience Las Vegas," she said, stroking his arm. She was having trouble keeping herself from touching him. He'd gotten a shower, too. He smelled *amazing*.

"Ah'd rather be home," he said, reaching over to stroke her hair which, luckily, was about the only thing that didn't hurt.

"We'll come back sometime."

Broch rolled his eyes. "Or nae."

Catriona read the signs to herself as they passed outside a big building.

A Special Gentleman's Club
Buffet Extravaganza
Wee Wedding Chapel

Catriona sat up.

No way.

That sign had to be a *sign*, right?

"Pull over."

The cab driver's gaze flicked to his rearview mirror. "I thought we were going to the airport."

"We are. But pull over. Go back. Make a U-turn."

Broch scowled. "Whit are ye doin'?"

Catriona grinned. "I have an idea."

"Aw, Catriona. Ah just wantae gae hame noo. Fast as possible. Ah don't even care we hae tae get on that infernal jet."

"I think you'll like this."

The cabbie made a U-turn and in a moment she saw her destination coming into view again. "Pull in here."

Broch peered out the window. "A church?"

"A chapel."

"A wedding chapel?"

She nodded. "Aye."

"Whose?"

"Ours."

Broch arched an eyebrow. "Ah don't remember askin'—"

She slapped his chest. "Yes you do. You've asked me like a million times."

"Ah think t'was more lik' twa times."

"Whatever. If twa means a *million*."

"And I don't remember ye ever sayin' aye."

"No. I didn't."

"Bit noo you're aff tae drag me tae the altar lik' a pregnant farmer's daughter?"

"What? Ew. No."

"Then whit are we doin' here?"

Catriona sighed as the taxi came to a stop in the parking lot. "Think of this as a dry run for the real thing."

"Ah dry run?"

"Yes. It won't be official, we won't get the paperwork done, but it will be fun and you can consider it a sort of promise from me."

"A *sort o'* promise. Ah loue the way ye modern fowk ne'er commit tae anythin'. Even a *promise* is *sort o'*."

Catriona reached for the handle of the taxi's door and immediately regretted stretching as her ribs ached. Pausing, she bobbed her head to try and catch a glimpse of herself in the rearview mirror.

Oh my.

Her lip was split. Something was off with her cheekbone too, though she couldn't quite place what. The rest of her body felt even worse.

"I hope there's not a swimsuit competition," she mumbled, sliding from the car.

She asked the taxi driver to wait and led Broch inside.

A man looked up from behind a counter, dipping his

magazine, but not fast enough for Catriona to *not* see it was a men's mag.

Classy.

"I didn't think they sold them anymore," she said, motioning to the magazine.

"Huh?"

"With the Internet and all."

The man snorted and put the magazine somewhere under the desk. "Can I help you?"

"We want to do the marriage thing."

He nodded. "Full photography and video?"

"Oh a few pics. No video. This isn't real. It's just a dry run. For fun."

"Uh-huh. Music?"

"Sure. I mean, the basics. Not a choir or anything. The wedding march bit."

He pushed a few sheets of paper in Catriona's direction. "Uh-huh. Sign here. Need a dress? Tux?"

Catriona concentrated on scribbling her name as the man pushed one sheet after the next at her while taking a few moments to glance at Broch.

He wore jeans.

That wouldn't do.

"You need to get your kilt."

Broch looked down at his legs. "Aye."

Before he could run outside the man caught his eye and pointed at him and then the paperwork. "You too."

Catriona handed Broch the pen and he scribbled his name before jogging out to the taxi.

A woman pushed aside a curtain separating the front area from the chapel. Her hair was dyed bright red.

"Are ye ready, me dear?" she asked.

Catriona chuckled. Having had to listen to Broch's heavy brogue for weeks on end, the woman faking her way through the accent sounded a little like the Lucky Charms leprechaun.

"Just a second, I have to wait for—"

Broch jerked open the door and entered in his kilt.

Catriona eyed him. "Did you get changed in the parking lot?"

He nodded.

She shrugged. A Scot dropping his drawers in public was surely not the most scandalous thing to happen in Las Vegas that week.

That *day*.

Probably that *minute*.

"Come with me meh sweeties, and I'll tack ye toooo da altar."

"She's speaking in your native tongue," whispered Catriona as they pushed through the curtain and followed the woman down the aisle. She couldn't help giggling. It had taken them hours to finish with the police after her ordeal. She was running on no sleep for over twenty-four hours and felt absolutely giddy.

Broch winced. "Whit she's sayin' is supposed tae be Scots?"

"I think so."

He snorted a laugh through his nose.

The woman stood behind a dais and motioned to the spot in front of it. "Have a stand der will ye? Where should we send yer pictures toooo?"

"Tae," mumbled Broch.

"What's that nooo?"

"Send the pictures *tae*. Not *toooo*."

The woman scowled and looked at Catriona. "What's your email?" she asked, effecting no accent at all.

Catriona covered her mouth to hide her giggles and rattled off her email.

The woman jotted it down.

"Did you come with vows?"

Catriona squinted at the woman. "*Vowels*?"

"*Vows*. Did you write your own vows?"

"Oh, no. Sorry. I'm, I'm really tired."

The woman nodded. "We get that a lot."

Broch looked at Catriona and took her hands in his.

"Are ye sure ye want tae dae this?"

A warm feeling flushed Catriona's cheeks as she realized she *did*.

She really *did*.

"When I thought I'd lost you I—"

Broch kissed her and she leaned in, feeling as if she could fall asleep that way, on her feet, her lips pressed against his.

When he pulled away she nearly fell forward.

I really have to get some sleep.

He sniffed and took her hand again, staring into her eyes. "Ah love ye, Catriona."

Catriona felt her own eyes begin to well. "I love you, too. It feels like we've known each other forever."

"Ah think mibbe we hae," he whispered. "Ah came through time tae find ye. Ah'm sure of it."

She touched his face. "And I was here, waiting for you."

"Holy shit." The woman pulled a handful of tissues from behind the dais. "You two are somethin' else." She blew her nose noisily into the wad and flipped a switch.

A fuzzy bagpipe version of the wedding march blared.

CHAPTER THIRTY-ONE

The elevator doors opened and Broch stepped through, Catriona draped in his arms. She'd fallen asleep shortly after downing three tiny bourbons on the plane, awoken briefly to disembark, and then fallen asleep again in the car on the drive home. He only needed to get her to her apartment and felt confident she'd be asleep again moments after he placed her in her bed.

"We should check in with Sean," she mumbled as he walked her down the hall to her door.

"Aye, we will."

She pulled on him to lift her face closer to his neck. She kissed him there, and he smiled.

"Whit are ye doin', sleepy lassie?"

"We're married now. I can do that anytime I want."

"Ye said it was fake."

"Close enough though, right?"

Broch lowered her feet to the ground and propped her against the wall beside her door. He stood close and she looked up at him, sliding her hands along his ribs to rest on his chest.

"Ravage me." Catriona said the words in a whisper but punctuated them with a giggle.

He pressed his lips to her forehead at her hairline.

Sae adorable.

"Ah would, but whit aboot all yer bruises?"

She looked up at him and touched her finger to her mouth. "I think my lips are good."

It was a lie. Volkov's fists had connected with her lips at least once, and the evidence remained. But Broch kissed her, as gently as his rising passion would allow and largely toward the right, undamaged side of her mouth. His hand slipped to the small of her back and drew her closer to him.

"Let's get ye tae bed."

"That's what ah'm talkin' about."

"For *sleep*. Ah'll join ye soon enough. Ye'll be tired o' me."

She scoffed. "I doubt it."

He heard a jingle and looked down to see she'd pulled her keys from her pocket.

"Open the door."

He took the keys and pushed them into the lock.

"Oh yeah, baby."

He looked at her, laughing. "Yer a nutter."

She giggled and thudded her head against his chest. "I am *so* tired."

He pushed open the door and bent down, slipping his arm behind Catriona's knees.

"Up we gang, lassie."

He lifted her and she wrapped her arms around his neck again.

"Aw, you're carrying me over the threshold."

Broch strode through the door and stopped upon spotting a pair of eyes staring at him from the sofa.

Sean sat there, watching television.

"Did I leave the TV on?" Catriona lifted her head from where it rested on his shoulder.

"What are you doing here?" she asked upon spotting Sean.

"Hello to you, too." Sean dipped to grab the remote and turn off the television. "Something wrong with your feet?"

Broch let her to the ground. "She's covered in a hundred bruises, bit ah think her feet ur fine."

Catriona tried to stand on her own but ended leaning on Broch, her head tilted back and eyes closed. "It isn't a hundred bruises. I did pretty well, considering. I messed him up good."

"Aye, ye did."

Sean's expression crinkled with concern. "Messed up, who?"

"We ran into a guy who likes beating up women. I had him on the ropes but Dez shot him. That was definitely more effective."

"Dez shot someone?" Sean rounded the sofa to inspect Catriona's busted lip. He sucked in a breath as he saw the extent of her injuries. "Who did this?"

"It's a long story. But the short version is he's dead and

Tyler's back. I think."

"He is. I saw him earlier." Sean sniffed. "Have you been drinking?"

Broch pinched the air. "She drank those wee bottles."

Catriona rolled her eyes. "Just a *few*."

"A few in the hotel 'n' a few oan the plane."

Sean grimaced. "It's six o'clock in the morning."

Catriona shrugged. "Not really. Not when you haven't slept in two days and spent half that time tied up in a basement watching women..." Catriona trailed off and walked toward her kitchen. "I could use a shot or two more, to be honest with you."

Sean looked at Broch. "Maybe you can tell me what's going on?"

Before he could start the story, Catriona interrupted.

"We're married now, y'know."

Sean looked from Broch to Catriona and back again. Broch shook his head.

"Nae really. T'was a lark."

Sean put his hand on his head. "I thought I came here to tell you a story, but now I think I need to hear what happened to—"

A new voice interrupted him.

"Sean, you're here. Thank *God*."

Broch felt the door bounce against his hip and turned to find Fiona standing in the doorway with their luggage, one piece in each hand.

Sean's agitation increased tenfold. "Fiona?"

"Fiona?" echoed Catriona as she straightened from where she'd been searching in the lower kitchen cabinet. Upon spotting Fiona, her lip curled. "You're in my house."

Fiona lowered the suitcases to her left and shut the door behind her. "He's *insane*."

Catriona leaned across the kitchen island. "Why are you in my house?"

Fiona scowled at Catriona and then looked at Sean. "What's wrong with her? She looks like she's been hit by a truck."

Sean shook his head. "The truck was me, actually. Who's insane?"

Catriona scowled at Sean. "Did you just say you were hit by a truck?"

Sean ignored her as Fiona answered.

"Rune's insane. He said he killed you."

Sean shrugged. "I suppose he did."

"*What?*" Catriona had been trying to climb on a barstool and she paused, teetering, wincing with the effort. Broch steadied her ascent and helped her position herself on the seat.

"Thank you," she whispered before addressing the group. "Can someone please tell me what's going on? And explain it to me like I'm brain dead because I pretty much am."

Sean frowned. "That's what I came to tell you. Rune came after me. Shot me. I ended up back in Scotland."

Broch perked. "Ye did?"

Sean smiled. "I did. I saw you as a baby again."

"Bit yer *here.*"

Sean glanced at Fiona. "I had help."

It was clear to Broch that Sean had more to say, but was reticent to say it in front of Fiona.

Seeming to sense the same thing, Fiona shook a finger at Sean.

"You don't have to hide any secrets from me, old man. I'm done with Rune. He tried to kill me. I barely got out alive. I slept in my trailer last night."

"Ha!" barked Catriona. She cleared her throat. "Sorry. That was louder than I meant it to be. But I'll take your *I slept in my trailer* and raise you an *I was tied up in an underground torture bunker.*"

Her eyes closed, head resting on her hand, her elbow on the breakfast bar propping up the lot. She snorted a tiny snore and then peeked at Broch with one eye. "I still don't know why she's in my apartment."

Broch stepped closer and put a hand on her shoulder to keep her from sliding off the stool.

"I came looking for you to tell you Sean is dead." Fiona tilted her head to the side. "Except he's not."

Sean shook his head. "I think we need to figure out what's going on here."

Catriona's breathing grew heavy and Broch put an arm around her. "Ah need tae put her in her kip."

Catriona snorted, her head snapping up. "What? No, I can't miss this. I'm awake. I'm awake." She rubbed her eyes and squinted at Fiona. "You're still here."

Fiona frowned. "I came to *warn* you."

"So you're saying we're all on the same side now?"

Fiona scoffed. "Well, don't get crazy. But I *did* stab Rune in the neck. Last I saw him he was on his knees in my parking lot, bleeding out."

"Is he dead? Did you see him disappear?" Catriona perked in her seat and toppled left. Broch caught and straightened her.

Fiona shook her head. "I don't know. I was busy getting away. But if he's not, I need you people to figure out how to kill him for good."

Sean sighed and sat on the arm of the sofa.

"Again," he said.

Catriona snored.

~~ THE END ~~

WANT SOME MORE? FREE PREVIEWS!

If you liked this book, read on for a preview of the next Kilty AND the Shee McQueen Mystery-Thriller Series!

THANK YOU FOR READING!

If you enjoyed this book, please swing back to Amazon and **leave me a review** — even short reviews help authors like me find new fans! You can also FOLLOW AMY on AMAZON

ABOUT THE AUTHOR

USA Today and Wall Street Journal bestselling author Amy Vansant has written over 20 books, including the fun, thrilling Shee McQueen series, the rollicking, twisty Pineapple Port Mysteries, and the action-packed Kilty urban fantasies. Throw in a couple romances and a YA fantasy for her nieces...

Amy specializes in fun, exciting reads with plenty of laughs and action -- she tried to write serious books, but they always ended up full of jokes, so she gave up.

Amy lives in Jupiter, Florida with her muse/husband a goony Bordoodle named Archer.

BOOKS BY AMY VANSANT

Pineapple Port Mysteries
Funny, clean & full of unforgettable characters

Shee McQueen Mystery-Thrillers
Action-packed, fun romantic mystery-thrillers

Kilty Urban Fantasy/Romantic Suspense
Action-packed romantic suspense/urban fantasy

Slightly Romantic Comedies
Classic romantic romps

The Magicatory
Middle-grade fantasy

FREE PREVIEW

KILTY SECRETS

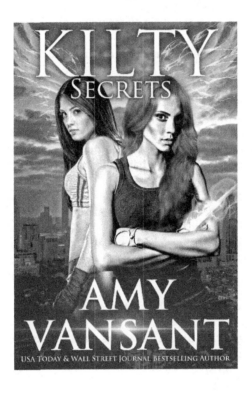

CHAPTER ONE

The message alert popped up at the bottom right corner of Balin's computer screen.

You've got a weird old-timey name, Balin. Maybe you weren't born in this century?

Balin scowled and responded with two capital letters.

FU.

His laptop dinged again.

I saw you were posting about changing the world. Survival of the fittest. Have you been going through a change?

Balin raised his fingers to type the weirdo a scathing retort and then paused. The person sending the messages had to have been cruising some very particular chat boards to be aware of his *survival of the fittest* posts.

Who is this? he typed instead.

The answer came back immediately, a message too long for someone to have typed so quickly. Balin imagined the stranger had copy-pasted it, which meant he was being trolled by someone who used the same lines on people, again and again, working off some twisted script. Maybe it was even a bot.

Ugh.

He was about to block the pest when another possibility occurred to him.

Maybe this person posts the same thing again and again because there are more people like me. Maybe this person is contacting all of us.

Could it be?

Balin glanced around the coffee shop to make sure no one was watching his reactions and then peered down at the message.

I can tell by your language you've been around if you know what I mean. Different times. I have too. I've got a new mission. I'm gathering our people to share this mission. The old times are over. It's time for us to make the world right. Make it stronger. The weak will perish.

Balin stared at the words, his fingers hovering over the

keys.

This was no bot.

There are more of us? he asked.

Many. I'm gathering an army. Will you join?

Balin scanned the room again. A girl sitting at a table across the room stared at him over her phone. She looked away as their gazes met.

She was holding her phone at an odd angle.

Is she taking a picture of me?

Balin leaped from his seat and ran to the girl to snatch the phone from her hands. She screamed, covering her face with her forearms as if expecting him to strike her.

"Who are you?" he asked.

Balin glanced at her phone screen. The girl *had* been chatting, but not with him. Something about slippers being on sale. A text from 'mom.'

She wasn't his mysterious stranger.

Feeling eyes, he scanned the room. A pair of girls and two baristas stood gaping at him like landed fish, frozen in their spots.

He tossed the girl's phone on the booth seat next to her, where it bounced once before settling on the edge. She whimpered and pushed herself against the back of the booth, wincing.

Balin took a moment to make eye contact with everyone in the shop.

"You're all gonna die."

One of the baristas was on her phone now. She'd shrunk down behind the counter trying to hide her call.

"You have no idea what's coming," he added.

He felt giddy.

Striding back to his seat, Balin typed without sitting down.

Where?

The answer appeared.

Los Angeles. Join us. We have a plan.

Balin smiled.

I'll be there.

He snapped the laptop shut and skittered out of the store as sirens blared in the distance.

CHAPTER TWO

Two years earlier, Los Angeles

"Hold it, Petrossian, *this* the place?" Officer Soto shoved the last of his hot dog in his mouth and brushed his hands together to rid himself of crumbs.

His partner scowled. "Yes. Do you have to be such a pig?"

"I'm hungry." Soto peered through the window of their cruiser at the large, square warehouse building beside them. "You sure this is it? Doesn't look like much is going on."

Petrossian shrugged and shifted the car into park. "That's what the map says. I don't argue with technology."

Soto hopped out of the vehicle, pretending to adjust his gun belt as he tugged at his underwear. He'd run out of clean boxer briefs and had resorted to wearing the Christmas boxers he'd found stuffed in the back of his drawer. The bunched leg had a death grip on his thigh. He made a mental note to do laundry when he got home.

"What's the problem?" he asked.

Petrossian shut his door and walked around the car to watch his partner pull at his underwear. "It looks like your underwear is riding up on you."

Soto thrust a thumb toward the building. "I mean what's the problem *here*."

"Oh. Possible 207."

Soto gave his boxers one last jerk before deciding the blood had returned to his right leg. "Okay. I guess, let's knock and see—"

Before they could take a step toward the entrance, the only door on the side of the metal building burst open, slamming against the outer wall and bouncing back into the face of a woman stumbling into the setting sun's rosy light. She raised both arms, one to block the door's ricochet and one to block the glare. Stumbling toward them, her voice cracked.

"Help me."

For a moment, Petrossian and Soto didn't move, both of them stunned by the girl's startling appearance. She wore a billowing white sleeveless shift, stained with what looked like fresh blood. The left shoulder strap of the tank dress had torn and flapped down, exposing her breast. Lacerations covered her chest and arms. Her blonde hair stuck matted to her forehead, stained by the same rusty crimson smears soiling her gown.

She staggered toward them, arms outstretched like the living dead.

"Holy shit," mumbled Soto.

Petrossian snapped from his daze and leaped forward to catch the girl as she collapsed into his arms.

"Call an ambulance. Call backup."

Soto fumbled with his shoulder mic and called in the requests.

"In there." The girl pointed at the building, her body shaking.

"Who? Who's in there? Is there someone else in there? Someone with you?"

She shook her head, her skull lolling on her neck as if the ability to keep her head upright had escaped her.

"*Him.*"

"Miss, help is on the way. What's your name? Can you tell me your name?"

"Cleo. Cleo Frye."

"She's that girl," said Soto, pointing at her. "The one who went missing."

Petrossian nodded and used his thumbs to raise the girl's drooping right eyelid.

"She's drugged."

"High?"

"*Drugged.*"

"I'm going in to look for more girls." Soto sprinted toward the door, gun drawn.

"Wait for backup!"

Soto pretended not to hear Petrossian's command. If there were more girls inside he wanted to be the first to find them. If this new girl had been kidnapped by the same guy who killed the others, he wasn't sure how much time anyone inside had.

I'm going to catch this bastard.

Cleo was the latest in a string of pretty young women to go missing over the previous year. They'd found the one before Cleo in an alley, dead, ten pounds lighter than when she'd disappeared, and that didn't include the weight of her severed fingers—nine of which they found in a bag tied around her neck. As with the girls before her, the pinky from her left hand was never recovered. The press had nicknamed him 'Pinky'. Although keeping fingers was one of his lesser sins, it was a constant.

Soto pulled open the door and peered inside, temporarily sun-blind. He heard Petrossian call again.

He took a deep breath and stepped into the darkness.

This stops now. On my watch.

He paused, listening, waiting for his eyes to adjust to the single bare bulb glowing in the otherwise inky space above him.

The only sound he heard was the cavernous space of the warehouse. The very silence of the chamber seemed to hiss in his ears. Though he felt the emptiness above him, walls flanked his left and right. He shuffled forward, gun held in front of him. A makeshift hallway of black-painted plywood led him toward a dark red curtain.

Soto groaned.

I don't like this.

In situations like these, nothing *good* ever waited behind a curtain.

Heart racing, he slid the heavy fabric aside. More low-watt bulbs hung overhead in this new space. The hallway continued forward. If only he could see *more—*

Flashlight. Duh.

Soto jerked his flashlight from his belt and held it beside his gun, pointing the way his bullet would fly should he spot the sick bastard who cut up those girls.

He crept forward, a step at a time, shining his light along the walls. He didn't like the feeling of being in a chute. He felt like a beef cow plodding to its death.

The air sounded different. Closer.

Shit. Up top.

He shone the beam skyward and found a black plywood ceiling a foot above his head. A few steps later, the ceiling opened again to the darkness. The warehouse's actual roof sat much higher than the occasional plywood planks appearing above him, straddling the makeshift walls.

Soto ran his flashlight along the next section of lower ceiling.

Anything could be going on up there.

The planks could be platforms for someone to stand. Checking corners and behind doors wouldn't be enough. He'd have to watch for attacks from above.

The flashlight's beam bounced off something shiny on the wall and Soto felt his finger flex on the trigger of his gun.

Jumpy.

A tangle of razor wire ran along the walls, constricting the path further, the network of silver mesh making it difficult to focus.

How had the girl escaped this hellhole?

The cuts.

That was why her dress and skin were torn. She must have run through the razor-wire-lined hall. The idea of it made his mouth dry.

Maybe I should have waited for backup. I should go back.

Soto heard a scraping noise and cocked his head to listen for the source.

Snap!

The popping sound flooded his veins with dread. Pain seared through the back of his ankle. As his leg collapsed beneath him, he spun on his good heel, roaring, frantic to find the cause of his agony.

Eyes.

His flashlight illuminated the face of an older man, staring up at him from the floor. The upper half of the man's torso protruded from the wall, in a spot the razor wire didn't cover.

There hadn't been a hole in the wall a minute before. Soto was sure of it. It was as if the man had opened a tiny door and slid himself through like a snake.

Light glinted off the large kitchen knife in the man's hand and Soto realized the awful truth.

He sliced my Achilles.

The man's eyes widened as Soto's gun trained on him. With his wispy, wild gray hair undulating like seaweed under the shaking glow of the flashlight, Soto's attacker made a strange grunting sound.

Soto's brain processed the man's problem before his ass even hit the ground.

He's stuck. The bastard slid out to cut me, and he can't get back in.

Soto's finger flexed.

I got you, you son of a—

Soto fired as he fell. He landed hard on the ground and a second shot rang out, this one high off the mark.

Fumbling to find his flashlight, Soto pointed it at the man.

The first bullet had struck his sneaky attacker in the chest. His eyes were wide and unmoving, the knife still in his hand.

With his good foot, Soto kicked at the knife. It remained in the man's hand, and he saw it was taped there.

Soto's breath came in short staccato bursts. Even with his foe apparently dead, he felt panic growing in his chest.

I have to get out of here.

There might be more of them. It didn't matter. He couldn't stand the darkness any longer—not with his foot disabled.

Soto tried to hop back down the hall, each bounce forcing a cry of pain from his lips. He gritted through it as far as he could and then collapsed to his belly, crawling like an animal toward the door.

He pushed open the door and wormed his way into the light, every inch of progress darkened by the prospect of someone grabbing him from behind.

Flashing lights hurt Soto's eyes as he crawled out. A blonde, ponytailed EMT hovered over the girl in the white dress. Another tech exiting the ambulance spotted Soto and strode in his direction.

"I got a cop!"

Time seemed to slow.

Petrossian stood from his crouched position at the head of the girl, his expression awash with concern, his gaze locked on Soto.

Soto heard the blonde EMT's voice before his brain processed the words.

"There's something strapped to this one's leg—"

Soto watched as Petrossian looked down at the kidnapped girl. His partner's eyes popped wide and he thrust out a hand as if to *grab* the EMT. As if to *stop* her.

"Don't touch—"

Sensing something was wrong, the second EMT stopped

his progress toward Soto and turned.

Soto covered his head as the world exploded with sound and light.

Get *Kilty Secrets* on Amazon!

ANOTHER FREE PREVIEW!

THE GIRL WHO WANTS

A Shee McQueen Mystery-Thriller by Amy Vansant

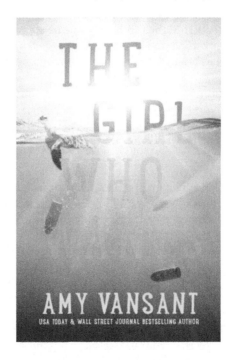

CHAPTER ONE

Three Weeks Ago, Nashua, New Hampshire.

Shee realized her mistake the moment her feet left the grass.

He's enormous.

She'd watched him drop from the side window of the house. He landed four feet from where she stood, and still, her brain refused to register the warning signs. The nose, big and lumpy as breadfruit, the forehead some beach town could use as a jetty if they buried him to his neck...

His knees bent to absorb his weight and *her* brain thought, *got you.*

Her brain couldn't be bothered with simple math: *Giant, plus Shee, equals Pain.*

Instead, she jumped to tackle him, dangling airborne as his knees straightened and the *pet the rabbit* bastard stood to his full height.

Crap.

The math added up pretty quickly after that.

Hovering like Superman mid-flight, there wasn't much she could do to change her disastrous trajectory. She'd *felt* like a superhero when she left the ground. Now, she felt more like a Canada goose staring into the propellers of Captain Sully's Airbus A320.

She might take down the plane, but it was going to *hurt.*

Frankenjerk turned toward her at the same moment she plowed into him. She clamped her arms around his waist like a little girl hugging a redwood. Lurch returned the embrace, twisting her to the ground. Her back hit the dirt and air burst from her lungs like a double shotgun blast.

Ow.

Wheezing, she punched upward, striking Beardless Hagrid in the throat.

That didn't go over well.

Grabbing her shoulder with one hand, Dickasaurus flipped her on her stomach like a sausage link, slipped his hand under her chin and pressed his forearm against her windpipe.

The only air she'd gulped before he cut her supply stank of damp armpit. He'd tucked her cranium in his arm crotch, much like the famous noggin-less horseman once held his severed head. Fireworks exploded in the dark behind her eyes.

That's when a thought occurred to her.

I haven't been home in fifteen years.

What if she died in Gigantor's armpit? Would her father even know?

Has it really been that long?

Flopping like a landed fish, she forced her assailant to adjust his hold and sucked a breath as she flipped on her back. Spittle glistened on his lips, his brow furrowed as if she'd asked him to read a paragraph of big-boy words.

His nostrils flared like the Holland Tunnel.

There's an idea.

Making a V with her fingers, Shee thrust upward, stabbing into his nose, straining to reach his tiny brain.

Goliath roared. Jerking back, he grabbed her arm to unplug her fingers from his nose socket. She whipped away her limb before he had a good grip, fearing he'd snap her bones with his Godzilla paws.

Kneeling before her, he clamped both hands over his face, cursing as blood seeped from behind his fingers.

Shee's gaze didn't linger on that mess. Her focus fell to his crotch, hovering a foot above her feet, protected by nothing but a thin pair of oversized sweatpants.

Scrambled eggs, sir?

She kicked.

He howled.

Shee scuttled back like a crab, found her feet and snatched her gun from her side. The gun she should have pulled *before* trying to tackle the Empire State Building.

"Move a muscle and I'll aerate you," she said. She always liked that line.

The golem growled, but remained on the ground like a good dog, cradling his family jewels.

Shee's partner in this manhunt, a local cop easier on the eyes than he was useful, rounded the corner and drew his own weapon.

She smiled and holstered the gun he'd lent her. Unknowingly.

"Glad you could make it."

Her portion of the operation accomplished, she headed toward the car as more officers swarmed the scene.

"Shee, where are you going?" called the cop.

She stopped and turned.

"Home, I think."

His gaze dropped to her hip.

"Is that my gun?"

GET *THE GIRL WHO WANTS* ON AMAZON!

Vansant Creations, LLC / Amy Vansant
Jupiter, FL
http://www.AmyVansant.com

Copy editing by Carolyn Steele
Proofreading by Effrosyni Moschoudi, Meg Barnhart & Connie Leap
Cover by Lance Buckley & Amy Vansant

Made in United States
North Haven, CT
12 February 2024

48629558R00117